Red Water

Jess Hanna is shanghaied aboard a whaling ship. Unlike most boys in the 1820's, Jess has no desire for the danger of a sailor's life, and he suffers greatly from the filth and backbreaking labor of the whaler. From the beginning, the voyage is beset by storms, accidents, and an evil scheme of the first mate to "lose" the ship and its cargo in the icy Antarctic Sea. But Jess, who never intended a whaler's career, grows to maturity during this time at sea and learns that justice is not easily attained.

RED WATER

By Robert Edmond Alter

WILDSIDE PRESS

To Ed—who wanted to go to sea

Contents

RABBLE ON A HILL

This bristling, brawling account of the days just prior to Lexington and Concord and through the Battle of Breed's Hill (commonly known as the Battle of Bunker Hill through the error of a British cartographer) should make history palatable.

TIME OF THE TOMAHAWK

"Pennsylvania in 1763 is the setting for swift-paced adventure as Whit learns of Pontiac's planned rebellion, is captured and later adopted by Indians, escapes, and survives many dangers to play a vital part in breaking the siege of Fort Pitt."

—*The Junior Literary Guild*

TWO SIEGES OF THE ALAMO

"This historical novel is based on the actual incidents connected with the dramatic battle of the Alamo and features Tack, an imagined character, which symbolizes all young Americans who fought and died in the battle. . . . Attractive maps and illustrations enhance the story and the author's note certifies the existence of all the characters with the one exception of Tack. Junior and Senior High School readers will be attracted by the intriguing style of this daring tale of the courage of early Americans."

—*Best Sellers*

WHO GOES NEXT?

Winner of the Gold Medal, Junior Book Award, 1967, Boys' Clubs of America, and a Junior Literary Guild selection.
"Twelve true and exciting tales of men in the 18th, 19th, and 20th centuries who attempted to escape just or unjust imprisonment. Although the men are not well-known, readers will long remember their remarkable, even unbelievable, ingenuity and courage as they sought freedom. Recommended."

—*School Library Journal*

Prologue

The sea was harder then—bigger, more remote. There was no machinery, no electricity, and harpoons were not fired from guns. Men had to look to themselves for help and to the seamen who toiled next to them; and every man—whether twelve or seventy, cabin boy or captain—was logged as a man and depended upon as such.

One mistake—just one moment of faltering courage—could leave a turbulent blotch of crimson froth and the scattered splinters of a whaleboat on the heaving sea.

Red water was tragic water when it was made from the blood of a boat's crew . . .

At the back of this book the reader will find a glossary of sea terms, an explanation of Pidgin English, and some notes on the authenticity of the whaling scenes described in the story.

1. You've Sailed Into Luck This Day

THE COMMODORE Mayo Tavern had a long porch fronting on the New Bedford waterfront with a rail about hip-high. Sitting with his feet cocked on the rail, Jess Hanna had a perfect view of the bustling activity of seaboard life. The crowded harbor was so clearly visible he might have been surveying it through a spyglass.

A hundred sail and more rode at anchor or were berthed at the wharves: stubby whalers, lordly Indiamen, clipper-built packets, battered coasters. Half a dozen nations were represented, but the majority of vessels floated the Stars and Stripes.

It was a fine sight, Jess thought, to see Old Glory so firmly entrenched upon the high seas once again. There

11

had been a time between 1808 and 1815 when the British had acted almighty chesty about America's freedom at sea. But the War of 1812 had solved all that, and now—seven years after the war—American ships and seamen were over the world's oceans like a horde of swimming ants.

Take the whaling industry alone; America now outnumbered all the rest of the whalers in the world, sailing a fleet of 700 ships, manned by 18,00 seamen. Yes sir, these were lively times!

But Jess himself didn't feel very lively. He slumped farther down in his captain's chair and let out a yawn, quite content to watch other people work for a change.

There was a whaler down at the dock right below the tavern, her great dolphin striker overhanging the wharf like a threatening spear. Jess gazed at her indolently.

She was the *Bunyan*—a bad-luck vessel, so they said. Her skipper, old Captain Morse, had been lost overboard rounding the Horn, and she herself had caught fire off the Cape Verdes with a full cargo of oil. Only the supreme effort of her crew had saved her from a holocaust death.

Lazily, Jess watched the sweating seamen laying back on the inboard end of a whip suspended from the whaler's main yard, hoisting aboard casks of provisions for her next voyage, which was scheduled for the morrow. The fat mound of beef and bread casks on the dock beneath the yardarm steadily diminished as the whip swayed load after load up to the yard, swung inboard and dropped down the *Bunyan*'s hatch.

A greasy voyage* to them, Jess thought, wishing the *Bunyan* well.

Mrs. Folger, the tavernkeeper's wife—spare and sparrowlike in build and movement, but with a crow's temper—came out on the porch and glared at the reclining Jess Hanna with her bird eyes.

"My sakes, Jesse," she snapped, "you go to get much lazier and you'll take root to that chair like a barnacle on a dock pile! Why ain't you up and about? There must be something you could find to do to earn your keep!"

Jess sighed and put his feet down and stood up.

"There ain't that much work to a stable like yours, Miz Folger," he said defensively. "I've already grained and curried that roan and cleaned up."

"Well, landsake, find *something* useful to do, can't you?"

Mrs. Folger was definitely against any form of idleness, believing that idle hands were mischievous hands.

"I swan," she went on irascibly, "if you grow a speck more worthless, we'll be able to stand you out in front of the tavern and use you for a statue!"

Mumbling to himself, Jess slouched off the porch and went around to the Commodore Mayo barn. It was true that he didn't do much around the tavern, but it was just as true that there wasn't much for a stableboy to do in a wharfside tavern that received most of its custom from seamen.

He gave the roan a short drink from the stable pail and then he washed the nag's eyes and nose with a

* See Glossary of Sea Terms.

damp rag and cleaned his ears for him, and decided to give him another going over with the corn brush. He thought about his life as he worked.

It hadn't been much, when you came right down to it. He was already seventeen and you couldn't say that he had made any great shakes of himself. He didn't know anything about his parents because he had been raised in an orphanage in Boston.

A farmer named Rapp, near Onset, had taken him out of the orphanage as an indentured apprentice when Jess was thirteen. But "indenture," Jess had quickly discovered, was only a mild legal word for slavery. Before the year was out, he had run away from the place, taking to a bleak and dreary country of scrub forest and cranberry bogs near Wareham.

A month of monotony and near starvation in the wilderness had forced him to take a job with the ferryman at Fairhaven. That hadn't worked out either. The ferryman used to drink a lot and then he would start seeing "hants" and have Jess up all night chasing them with a stick.

One night the poor man became so haunted he took a horse pistol to the ghosts— and Jess had the hant-stick shot right out of his hand. He left the ferryman.

He was trudging wearily along the waterfront in New Bedford one day when Elihu Folger stepped into the tavern yard and called to him.

Elihu was a fat, kindly, henpecked man and he had asked did Jess know how to mind horses, because his other stableboy had run off to be a whaleman. If Jess would mind the tavern barn and help out in the tap-

room when business got rushed, then Elihu would pay
him eleven dollars and board. Jess had been there ever
since.

He liked the place well enough—except for Mrs.
Folger's crabbing. There wasn't much work for one
thing, and the food was good for another, and he had
a snug little room to himself in the barn. He figured
to stay there for a while longer.

Jess put a measure of oats and a fork of bluejoint in
the manger for the hungry-looking roan, and then he
pitched some hay into the manger of one of the empty
stalls and lay down in it to treat himself to a short nap.

Jess opened his eyes. Voices were in the barn, but
at the far end. He could barely pick up a few words.

" . . . always bearing in mind it must be a full cargo.
Otherwise the game isn't worth the candle because . . ."

Jess peeked over the edge of the bin.

Three men were standing in the blue shadows near
the end stall. He knew all three of them by sight. One
of them, Jack Hay, was staying at the Commodore
Mayo. He was the cockney steward off the *Bunyan*.

The second man was the *Bunyan*'s first mate, Mr.
Starr, the man always referred to as *the* mate. A tall
broad man with a hard, jutting jaw. He was known
as a bucko mate.

The third man was Mr. Munro, the owner of the
Bunyan; a fat, squat little man, bent of shoulder and
short in the right leg. His narrow, pointed chin tended
to meet his pendulous nose and his light blue eyes were

strange in the darkness of his sallow face. He seemed
to be doing most of the talking.

Jack Hay gave a start and caught at Starr's right
arm—an arm that ended in a long steel hook instead
of a hand. The mate's hand, Jess had heard, had gone
to a sperm whale in the Arctic sea. Wordlessly, Hay
pointed toward Jess's stall.

Mr. Munro's reaction was as abrupt as a slammed
door. He gave a start, spun on his heel and hurried out
of the barn. Mr. Starr, however, was made of sterner
cloth. He didn't like to run from anything. He took a
step toward Jess.

He had a swart complexion, a heavy-jowled counte-
nance and a bulbous nose that shone like a battle
lantern. But it was his eyes that riveted Jess's attention.

They were as blue and cold as the water on the New-foundland banks when the icebergs came wallowing south from the Greenland glaciers.

Without warning, those eyes became human. The hard features relaxed in a tight smile.

"Gut me," he said in a quarterdeck-booming voice. "We've picked up a pilot fish, Jack. You hear all you want to hear, my son?" he asked Jess. "You didn't miss anything important, did you?"

"I didn't hear anything, mister," Jess said, climbing out of the manger. "Your talk just woke me up. I'm no Jack Pry."

"Good!" the mate said. "That's the breed for me. A likely lad, eh Jack? Do 'ee mark the height and heft of him? He'd make a strokesman or I'll drink bilge!

What do you say, bucko? How would you take to ship-ping out? We're shorthanded, we are."

"In a whaler?" Jess had to scoff. A whale ship was the seaman's horror. A dirty, greasy, dangerous, back-breaking way to go to sea. And few voyages were ever under two years duration; three was the average.

"No, thanks, mister," he said. "I know when I'm well off. You can save your stove boats and your stinking trypots for somebody with a strong back and a weak mind."

He took a step out of the stall and started to go by the big mate. In a flash of blurred steel Starr's hook whipped out and snagged a bunch of Jess's shirt, hold-ing him pinioned. The mate's blue eyes froze into chips of ice.

"It won't do, my son," he said raspingly, "to mock the whaling industry. You mock George Starr when you do, and——"

"George!" Jack Hay said entreatingly, tugging at Starr's hook arm. "Belay it, George, 'E's a right lad, 'e is. Let 'im alone."

The mate, still staring into Jess's taut face, nodded and withdrew his hook.

"You've sailed into luck this day, my son," he said tauntingly. "Best not push it."

Jess had no intention of pushing his luck. Perhaps he had smelled trouble where no trouble was brewing. But that clandestine meeting of the mate, the steward and the owner needed explanation. However, this was not the time or place for it. For a vivid moment there,

he had thought that lightning-swift hook was going
right into his ribs.

He hurried out of the barn, relieved to find himself
still in one piece.

A familiar, friendly world waited outside the barn.
Loaded drays and wains trundled in and out of the
open warehouses. In every cooperage the clatter of
maul against hoop and stave resounded, and the clang
of sledge on glowing iron rang in every smithy. The
song of brown hemp and golden manila fiber spinning
into stout cable or flexible harpoon line hummed in
the ropewalks. Seamen ranged up and down the docks.

Four men had drifted into the Commodore Mayo's
yard. One of them carried a twelve-foot barb-headed
harpoon over his shoulder, the earmark of the whaleman. A burly seaman hailed Jess as he was starting
up the porch steps.

"Will 'ee hove to, laddy buck, and answer a man's
question?"

"Sure." Jess had to smile. He loved to listen to an
Irish brogue.

"Can you be telling us where we'll find the mate o'
the *Bunyan* now? They tell us he's after being about
this tavern somewhere."

"Back in the barn," Jess said, turning to point.

The mate and Jack Hay were just then coming
through the barn doors—and a strange thing happened.
Jack Hay took one look at the little cluster of seamen in

the distant yard and stopped dead. Then he turned off to the right without a word to Starr and vanished.

"These men are looking for you," Jess told Starr as the mate came around the end of the porch.

The mate's hard eyes roved coldly over the mute seamen.

"Looking for berths, eh?" he said shortly. "You with the harpoon! Are you what you look to be, or do you just carry that thing around to pick your teeth with?"

"Jekiel Burr, sir!" the seaman said smartly, tugging at his forelock in the prescribed manner. "I be a harpooner out of Martha's Vineyard."

"You'll do," Starr said gruffly. He looked at the Irishman.

"Gypo Barnaby, sur. A whalerman out of the auld country, so I am."

"A Mick peat-bogger." Starr grinned wolfishly. "I've never shipped an Irishman yet that wasn't trouble."

"Me, sur?" Barnaby looked appalled by the thought. "Sure, I'd ruther cut me mither's throat than give a skipper that much trouble!" He held up a little pinky to show exactly now much *that* meant.

"Yes you would," Starr said. He looked at the third man, a husky young Polynesian with black hair that curled crisply to his scalp, with a delicately chiseled nose and pale eyes that contrasted strangely with his dark face.

"I fella Tavi," the Polynesian said. "Fella me row one big fella boat along wind. You savvy?"

"Kanaka, eh?" Starr said. "Well, you've the arms on you for an oar, my son. But time will tell whether you can outrow the wind. All right. I'll ship the lot of you. 'Way smartly for the ship now, and you'll sign articles."

The seamen shoved off and Starr started after them. Then he paused to glance back at Jess. It was a look which ought to have stuck at least four inches out of Jess's back.

2. Decided to Grow Sea Legs
After All, Did You?

THE USUAL seaman crowd filled the taproom that night and Jess helped Elihu and Bet, the colored serving girl, behind the counter. Gypo Barnaby was there and he seemed to take a fancy to Jess. Whenever Jess wasn't busy with the glasses, Barnaby would have a gam with him.

He had seen some rare sights at sea, had Barnaby; mutiny, piracy, cannibals, stove boats, typhoon and shipwreck.

"Have 'ee heard of the *Essex* now? Sure and it happened but two years back! A whaler she was out of Nantucket. And it's herself spotted spouts whilst cruising the Pacific Ocean. Well then, she lowered boats and gave chase to a shoal of sperm whales. Ere long a ruddy great monster whale came out of the shoal and bore down on the ship directly. *The ship*, mind 'ee! Not the whaleboats.

"Well then, this ruddy great spermacetty dashed his head against the hull of the ship, so he did. And again and again! So that in ten minutes by the clock the hull opened up and the sea rushed in and the poor ship went down. And not a spar nor plank of her have they found to this blissed day!"

"A whale did that?" Jess marveled. "To a full-rigged ship?"

"Losh! I've seen whales chew up boat and crew like t'was naught but a plug of tobacco, so I have!" Barnaby avowed. "It's great terrible beasts they are!"

He upped his cup and drained a dram of rum without wincing—which Jess figured was quite a trick. Then he smacked his lips and leaned his head toward Jess in a confidential manner.

"This *Bunyan* now. I do hear she has a bad name?"

"That's what they say," Jess said. "She lost her skipper last voyage. Captain Morse, an old Bedford whalerman."

"Aye," Barnaby muttered, "I've heard of Morse. And fire in the hold, they say the *Bunyan* had. And her on the track home! Aye—an ill ship, and no mistake!"

Jess looked at the Irish seaman with a wondering smile.

"I'll be curried with a brick if I can understand why you'd want to sign articles aboard such a ship, Gypo."

"Bliss me, me bhoy! Don't 'ee know that an Irishman follows trouble the way a calm follows a squall?

Sure and we're attracted to it, ye might say, like a magnet!"

Jack Hay slipped into the taproom and stationed himself at a remote corner table. He made a sign to Jess to fetch him a drink.

He was the type of man that Jess had learned to distrust; small, ferret-faced—quick smile, quick voice, quick eyes—all of it sudden, like the snapping of fingers.

"Any *Bunyan* seamen in 'ere tonight, Jesse lad?" Hay asked, his eyes darting here, there, like swallows trapped in a barn.

"No. Only that new hand—Barnaby."

"Oy see, oy see," Hay said rapidly, never once looking directly at Jess. "Leave us alone now."

Jess shrugged and walked away. If Hay wanted to be left alone, it suited him. But a surprise awaited him that night when he reached his little room in the barn. Jack Hay was sitting on Jess's bed with a pocket pistol in his hand.

"Close the door," Hay said.

Jess closed the door and set the candle-holder he was carrying on his foot locker. He looked at Hay. It was apparent that the little cockney was scared to death. But of what?

"Look, Hay," Jess said, "I took about all the bilge I want off your mate today. I don't know what you think you're doing in here, but clear out. I'm tired and I want some sleep."

Hay wagged his little pistol impatiently.

"Jesse, oy've a fyvor to arsk of you. You'll be a good lad, now won't 'ee? You'll 'elp a poor seaman that's gone onto a leeshore. Certain you will! And 'ere—" digging in his pocket and coming up with a sovereign— "'ere is a bit of something to bind the bargain, like."

Jess looked at the gold coin but didn't touch it.

"What am I supposed to do for that?"

"Let me sleep 'ere like a good lad. 'Ere in yer room. Just for this night. All right?"

Jess shrugged and took the coin. It was no skin off his nose if Hay wanted to sleep in the barn instead of in his own room in the Commodore Mayo. Then, against his will, a sudden sense of compassion came over him and he started to give the coin back.

"Look, Mr. Hay, you seem to be in some sort of trouble. Maybe I could help you in—"

"No no no!" Hay wagged the pistol again. "It aren't any of yer business, myte."

Jess gave it up and turned to the door.

"All right. But I'll be sleeping in the manger right by here if you need me."

Jess went out of the room and found the pitchfork in the dark and dumped some hay into a bin and climbed in after it. For a while he tried to center his drowsy night-thoughts on Jack Hay.

The man is almighty afraid of something. And he's got a suspicious relationship going with the first mate and the owner of the *Bunyan*. And what on earth could give a mere steward the right to refer to a first mate by his given name? George . . . George . . . Starr . . .

with a hook for a hand . . . a hookarmed bucko
mate . . .

Exactly what it was that woke him he would never
know. A knock, a struggle, a cry in the night.

Suddenly he was awake and sitting bolt upright. It
was still dark. Pitch-black in the barn. He could hear
the roan stamping nervously two stalls down. Something had roused him too. What?

Jess climbed out of the manger and stood in the stall
in a mood of indecisive bewilderment—stupid with
sleep. Then he remembered where he was and that
Jack Hay had rented his room for the night. He went
to the door and opened it but couldn't see anything for
the pre-dawn blackness that filled the little room like
the bottom of a deep well.

"Hay?" he whispered. "Hay?"

There was no answer. Jess felt his way to the foot
locker and fumbled around until he found his tinderbox. He struck a spark and got the candle going.

He straightened up and looked at the bunk and
jumped back a good foot, his heart going bump in his
throat.

Jack Hay was crammed down in the sideboard bed
on his back with his eyes and mouth wide open. The
pitchfork, which Jess had used earlier, was sticking
out of the steward's narrow chest like Triton's tined
spear.

Jess backed softly out of the room and started
through the barn door, which was just beginning to
square off the first faint gleam of sea dawn. There was

a quick movement somewhere near him. Jess whirled —and met a brilliant, abrupt shattering of consciousness.

He came to life in a sort of quiet confusion.

They were all around him in the dark. He could not see them at first, but their low, guarded voices were a murmuring fact. Very slowly, Jess opened his eyes. He was aware of three things: a splitting headache, a strange fishy stench, and a rolling movement that sickened his equilibrium.

His eyeballs moved in little puddles of pain, and he seemed to hear his eyelids open and close as if they were paper. A thick matting of dried blood and hair thatched the back of his throbbing head.

His eyes swam into focus and he saw that he was sprawled over empty casks in the hold of a ship. Four other equally bewildered men were in there with him. He sat up and rubbed his hands together. They, and everything about him, seemed to be covered with a fine coating of grease.

A whaler, he thought blankly. *I've been shanghaied aboard a whaler!*

It was an old old practice—shanghaiing; though it hadn't always gone by that exact name. They rendered a man insensible—by drugs or blows—in order to ship him forcibly on a vessel needing sailors. It was the work of crimps—the agents who procured seamen by fair means or foul (mostly foul). But Jess had an idea that he hadn't been shipped by a crimp.

The four men in the hold with him all had the unmistakable look of hayseed about them, and he figured they were innocent farmboys who had wandered into town for the weekend and had fallen into the coercing hands of the crimps.

"Wull, what's happened here?" a pie-faced man asked bewilderedly. "Where are we?"

"In the hold of a whaler," Jess told him. "We've been shanghaied."

Evidently they weren't such bumpkins that they didn't know what it meant. None of them had to ask, at any rate. They looked outraged, confused and frightened. Jess felt the same way.

"C'mon," he said. "Let's find the captain."

He had a strong suspicion, though, that they were too late. That roll he felt under his feet suggested that the ship had already parted from the land. They went through a door into an after compartment and up a companionway leading to the waist.

On deck they were greeted by a bedlam of noise—the creak of sheets and braces racing through a multitude of creaking blocks as fore and aft, alow and aloft, on every mast the heavy canvas fell from the yards and the yards were braced sharp over to put the ship on the starboard tack. The crew—mostly red-eyed from a last carouse—was kept hopping by a crackling series of orders issued from the poop.

Jess and the other shanghaied men hurried to the nearest bulwark and gawked at the water that separated them from the receding harbor.

Free of the wharf, divorced from bondage to the land, the ship became a living thing, gliding with the current but not dependent on it, sensitive to the least pressure on the wheel and the efficiency with which her towering canvas was set.

New Bedford diminished rapidly astern, the green tongue of Sconticut Neck faded into the heat haze to larboard, the ship's helm was put over and she went about on the starboard tack for the run out of Buzzards Bay.

Jess reached for a shroud. He was a good swimmer. There was still a chance he could reach the shore.

"Belay that!" a voice roared.

The five shanghaied men turned and saw a man holding a boarding pistol on them. He was evidently one of the mates.

"I'll shoot the man that tries to jump this ship," he said.

The pie-faced man lumbered forward like an angry bear and started to make an outraged protest.

"Looky here, mister, you can't—"

The officer swung the barrel of his pistol and clipped the pie-faced man on the point of his chin. It was a neat blow. It knocked Pie-face to the deck.

"Looky here ain't my name!" the officer shouted at the cowed men. "It's Gant! I'm third mate. You'll say *sir* when you step in my shadow, and you'll tack a mister to my name. Now fall aft! Jump—blast you!"

They jumped.

A big man was standing with his back to them in the alleyway between the two small cabins in the stern, evidently studying the *Bunyan*'s wake. When he suddenly turned around, he looked right into Jess's face —and smiled.

"Well, my son," Starr said, "changed your mind, eh?

Decided to grow sea legs after all, did you? Aye, you've come to the right ship and the right man to learn you how."

"We demand to see the captain!" Jess said angrily. "You can't shanghai us and get away with it!"

"Shanghai?" Starr's eyes widened. He looked at the third mate. "Were these men shanghaied aboard, Mr. Gant?"

"No, sir," Gant said, smiling thinly. "They're stowaways."

"Oh, well then," Starr said. "that puts it in another light. Stowaways *should* see the captain. That's only proper." He motioned with his hook toward one of the small stern cabins.

"All right, you slime!" he roared at them. "Lay alow!"

Anticipating the worst, Jess started aft around the skylight. Gypo Barnaby was at the helm and he barely turned his face toward Jess to tip him a wink. Jess led the way down the companion.

Four staterooms opened off the companionway. The main cabin itself was as commodious as the Commodore Mayo's kitchen, with a central table and benches, a long settee under the stern windows, and a glittering arms-rack around the butt of the mizzenmast.

There was a little bent old man, with a goatlike white beard, eating a bowl of mush at the table. He was in a nightshirt and nightcap and Jess thought he was a passenger at first.

"Captain Coffin," Starr said to the old man, "these lubbers was found in the hold. Stowaways, sir."

Captain! Jess was amazed. This decrepit old man drooling mush in his beard was the skipper of the *Bunyan*?

Captain Coffin's moist eyes blinked vaguely at the group of men.

"Yes? Yes? What is it?" he said testily. "Can't you see I'm trying to eat my porridge, Mr. Mate?"

"I said they're stowaways, sir," Starr repeated.

Jess pushed forward. "It's not true! We were shanghaied!"

"Shanghaied? Shanghaied?" the old man mumbled in his mush. "What is this talk of shanghaiing, Mr. Mate?"

"Nothing to it, sir," Starr said. "I know the trick. It's an old dodge, but it won't wash here. They stow away, and when they're caught at it they claim they was shanghaied and refuse to work."

"It's a lie!" Jess insisted. "We were—"

"Please, please!" Captain Coffin said, spluttering flakes of mush over the table. "I am not feeling well. I haven't been to sea in some years and I've yet to recover my sea legs."

He stood up, as bent as a little gnome, and wagged a vague hand at Starr.

"You attend to it, Mr. Mate. Take charge of the ship."

"Aye aye, sir," Starr said, grinning savagely. "You can leave everything in my hands. I'll sort it out Bristol fashion."

The old man picked up a whalebone-knobbed cane and hobbled into his stateroom with it. Starr turned and opened a drawer in a sideboy with his hook. Then he placed a copy of the ship's articles on the table.

"Every man jack in this cabin is going to sign them articles," he said, and there was an ugly look in his cold eyes. "If he don't, I'll sling him in irons and he'll rot in the lazarette for the rest of the voyage. And should I hear just one more word about anybody being shang-haied—I'll stomp his blasted carcass out of shape! Now sign!"

Jess became conscious of a new and unfamiliar sensation. For the first time since he had left the orphanage someone was trying to coerce him with threats into doing something he didn't want to do. He reacted with angry, obstinate refusal.

"I won't sign."

That strange icy gleam came into Starr's eyes.

"I think you will, my son," he said. "It's mutiny to refuse an officer's orders."

Jess drew a deep breath. His stomach felt hollow and his heart was thudding rapidly. The blood tingled away from his face.

"I won't sign."

"Do you know how we treat mutineers?" Starr asked. "We—"

Again the hook caught him unaware—snagging in his belt and snatching him straight into Starr. Something black flashed in the mate's left hand and exploded in Jess's head.

He dropped into another pit of unconsciousness.

3. The Devil Is Laying Eggs

THE KANAKA Tavi was bending over him when he came around. Jess looked around and found he was in a grubby bunk in the crowded fo'c'sle. A handful of off-watch seamen were sleeping and snoring in tiered bunks. The place had a fetid, briny smell like old seaweed.

"Fella head belong you walkabout too much?" Tavi asked him.

"Aye," Jess muttered ruefully, feeling his second bump. "Wonder what he hit me with—one of the anchors?"

"All fella mate carry one fella stick, smash'm fella head altogether."

"Altogether is right!" Jess agreed. He sat up and

looked at the young Kanaka. "Where did you learn to speak pidgin English, Tavi? On whaleboats?"

Tavi shook his head. "All fella sailor come along island belong my home. Fella me belong Rapa."

"Rapa Island?"

The third mate's voice boomed down the fo'c'sle hatch— "On deck all the starbowlines!"—and the Kanaka turned away to tumble up topside with the new watch.

The old watch stumbled below and made thankfully for their bunks. One of them was the pie-faced man who had been cracked on the jaw by Gant. He looked as though he were ready to drop.

"Better get on deck, Hanna," he said. "The mate's looking for you."

"I'm surprised I'm not in irons," Jess said. "I didn't sign the articles."

"That's what you think," Pie-face said. "The mate put down your name and an X after it and touched the pen to your hand. Seems that's legal, as far as sea law's concerned."

Huh! Live and learn, Jess thought. He went topside.

The second mate's name was Ralls. He was a dapper man with a reflective face that somehow did not seem to belong on a rough whaler. He pointed at Jess with the stem of his whalebone pipe.

"Lay aloft, Hanna. We're setting more sail."

Jess wet his lips and looked up at the towering white pyramids of canvas. They reached so far above him they seemed to be scraping the azure bottom of the sky with their trucks. Ralls glanced at him with a touch of compassion.

"Barnaby!" he called. "Take the lubber up and show him the ropes."

Jess could have gladly shook Mr. Ralls's hand—if such a thing had been allowed.

It was noon and the ship was footing it nimbly for the open sea, Nantucket and the speck of No Man's Land somewhere out of sight to larboard, Block Island over the starboard horizon.

From his station on the main yard, with his bare toes desperately clutching the footrope and both hands clinging for all he was worth to the yardarm, Jess could get a more expanded view of the *Bunyan*.

She was bigger than he had anticipated—a 300-ton bark. She had ample bows and a full waist. There was very little rake aft to her masts as she had not been designed for speed. She usually cruised at about seven knots. Her bulwarks were high and massively built and pierced for one twelve-pound carronade a side.

"Gypo!" Jess called to Barnaby on the other end of the main yard. "I thought this was a whaler. Why do we need those guns?"

"Sure and there's many an occasion in the Solomons when a battery comes in handy. Cannibals and headhunters, do 'ee see? And there's still some pirate lads about in the Indian Ocean."

The Solomons and headhunters, the Indian Ocean and Malay pirates. The words sloshed around in Jess's mind like a mist of glory, all lush and fat and colorful, and his imagination sideslipped and he saw a glint of sun on a far lonely shore and heard the play of cutlasses and spears and the sudden crashing belch of a cannon . . . .

For the first time in his life Jess realized that adventure was all around him; the mysteries of life lay close-packed, uncountable as grains of sand on the sea's shores. They had walked beside him, unseen and unheard, calling out to him, asking why he was deaf to their crying, blind to their wonder. But now the veil had dropped from his eyes.

All right, he decided. He would settle down, learn to be a seaman, and make the most of it. He would turn a new leaf, as the old saying went.

It wasn't easy. The mazelike mystery of brails and braces, halyards and topping lifts, sheets and tacks, stunsails and staysails, shrouds and spars and all the line in the standing and running rigging were enough to make his head spin. And it all had to be learned on his own time—of which he was given very little.

Whalermen liked to keep a clean ship: at least on topside. All the *Bunyan*'s gear had to be kept taut and neatly flemished down, her boats and all their equipment in order, her decks scrubbed and swabbed, her rigging and sheets and halyards overhauled, the bilge sounded, the pumps tested, the boats caulked, and painting and tarring and more and more scrubbing, watch and watch during the night, four hours on and four hours off, and catch a dash of broken sleep when you could.

And, always, the mate's angry cry down the fo'c'sle hatch:

"All hands on deck! Shake a leg below!"

George Starr was like Mrs. Folger in that he too believed that idle hands were mischievous hands; so they holystoned the decks over and over again, until they were immaculate and bone-white, and Starr and Gant helped them at their toil by bellowing an endless stream of blasphemous oaths in their ears, and lashed at them with a rope's end to hurry them along.

Ride 'em, drive 'em, haze 'em! It was the American whaler's way of life. An old saying had it that soft treatment and bad food was the British way, and hard treatment and good food the American way. But not on the *Bunyan.* Hard treatment and bad food was their lot. Their diet never varied. A wedge of salt junk, a biscuit as tough as flint, and something called "Long-lick" molasses. Sickening as it was, there was never enough of it. The men always went on deck hungry. Another of Starr's mottos was: Full stomachs make slow sailors.

The *Bunyan* carried three harpooners, and they were logged as petty officers. They ate and slept aft with the mates and helped in the hazing and punishment; and they were good at that sort of thing, being for the most part men of limited intelligence.

If a seaman was a laggard the harpooners went at him with rope-ends. If a man talked back to an officer or even looked surly at one, the harpooners and mates pounded him into the deck with their fists and boots. And if a man broke any of the numerous sea rules, he was triced up by his thumbs in the weather rigging in such a manner that when the ship was upright his toes touched the deck, but when she rolled his whole weight was suspended on his thumbs. Then one of the burly harpooners would give him a dozen lashes with an improvised cat-o-nine-tails.

Mr. Ralls, however, was of a different stamp. He didn't believe in hazing, and Jess had never seen him strike a seaman. Jess had the wheel one night as the old spouter went hammering along close hauled through head seas in the darkness, and Mr. Ralls was standing the deck watch.

A whaler was different in design than other ships in that it had a boxlike stern with a small cabin set on either side, used for housing the whaling paraphernalia. A deck stretched across the cabins to roof in the alleyway below, which contained the wheel and the skylight. This arrangement protected the helmsman from the sun and rain and heavy seas, but being open at both ends it made a breezy place to have to stand a four-hour night trick at the wheel.

Passing by the helm for a glance in the binnacle, Ralls noticed that Jess was shivering in his cotton shirt.

"Don't you have a jacket, Hanna?" he asked.

"No, sir. All I was wearing when I decided to stow away on this ship was my pants and shirt."

Ralls's face looked like a rare minted coin whose stamping had become blurred and undecipherable, and when he smiled his face seemed to take on a sad aspect. He smiled now.

"Careless of you," he said jocularly. Then he turned

serious. "Whalers usually don't shanghai hands who
are working in a dockside establishment. They prefer
visiting farmers who can't be traced so easily. I wonder
why Starr decided to lift you?"

"To shut my mouth, I think, sir," Jess said levelly.
He had an idea that Ralls was a man who could be
trusted and he decided to take a chance and confide
in him.

"I overheard Starr and Jack Hay and Mr. Munro
having a secret meeting in the tavern barn the day before we sailed."

"Eh? They were talking with the owner?"

"Aye. Mr. Munro told Starr to bear in mind that it
must be a full cargo; otherwise the game wouldn't be
worth the candle. But that didn't make much sense
to me, and still doesn't."

"A full cargo," Ralls muttered bemusedly. "The
game wouldn't be worth the candle . . ." He pursed
his lips and drew out his pipe, stared into the bowl.

"It sounds as if the devil's laying eggs," he said. "But
what they'll hatch I can't imagine."

He took a turn about the poop and came back to
the wheel.

"And you say the steward was with them? I wonder
now if that had anything to do with his disappearance?"

Jess glanced at the binnacle and corrected his
course.

"Jack Hay didn't disappear, sir," he said. "He was
murdered the same night I was shanghaied."

"Murdered!"

"Yes, sir. Somebody shoved a pitchfork in his chest in the tavern barn."

"But not Starr surely! Not if Hay and Starr were in cahoots somehow with the owner?"

"I don't know, sir. It doesn't make sense to me either. All I know is, Hay was scared to death of something."

There was no chance for further talk. Evidently the old man had been watching the telltale that swung from a beam in the main cabin. This was the cabin compass and by it the captain could tell the course without going on deck. The companion door opened in the larboard house and old Captain Coffin peered out of the darkness with a malevolent expression.

"You're off course!" he cried in a cackle voice, pointing his cane at Jess. "I'll have you logged for incompetence! Mr. Ralls, you're in command of the deck! Can't you see that the ship follows a true course? Why must everything be left up to me? Why can't I expect and receive assistance from my subordinates?"

He turned away, his querulous voice dragging after him, enumerating all his trials and tribulations—childlike and rather pathetic.

Eight bells rang, sharp and clear and in metallic pairs. The midwatch was over. A seaman named Ezekiel Whitney came aft, tugging his forelock to Mr. Ralls, and relieved Jess at the wheel.

The second mate was standing by the starboard mizzen shrouds when Jess went by him. All he said was—"Keep a close tongue on what you've told me,

Hanna. It will all out soon enough in the wash, I suspect."

"Aye aye, sir," Jess said.

But it was the cleaning of that dirty wash that was starting to concern him. It had suddenly activated a rather unhappy trend of thought. If Starr had shang-haied him to shut his mouth—how could Starr afford to let him return to New Bedford at the end of the voyage?

4. A Dead Whale Or A Stove Boat

THERE WERE times when Jess couldn't decide whether his bumpy mattress was stuffed with old corn-cobs or with broken crockery. But this was not one of those times. In the brisk pre-dawn darkness of half-sleep the mattress felt as soft as down.

It was like pulling teeth to have to leave his warm bunk when the mate's call thundered over the dog-weary men in the fo'c'sle.

"Turn to the starbowlines! Lively, blast you! Lively!"

"Sure and I'd sell me soul to the devil for one hour more of sleep, I would that" Barnaby grumbled, reaching for his seaboots.

Jess said nothing because he couldn't decide whether he would sell his soul for an hour's worth of sleep or for a square meal. The decision seemed too profound for a snap judgment.

A cutless moon sank down the sky and bathed the bark in the cold radiance of its beams. Dawn, yet unseen, was on the way. The constellations marched and wheeled across the dark blue vault and the whaler's riding lights twinkled and dimmed in the ethereal light. The sea beyond the bulwarks was so still that the liquid parings from the cutwater did not break or foam as they rolled away from the bows.

The look on Starr's face was as chill as a glacier illuminated by moonbeams, and Jess had an idea that the mate must have been fighting some personal devil in his cabin with a bottle, before he turned out the watch. He began to wonder if Starr was, perhaps, a little mad.

From the masthead came a prolonged, intoned cry in the dark.

"Sail oooh!"

There was a bustle of activity, the slap-slap of bare feet on the deck as seamen rushed to the bulwarks and the shrouds, and Starr's call:

"Where away?"

"Dead ahead and on the larboard bow!"

Jess sprang into the larboard main shrouds and stared out at the motionless silver-shot sea. There was a long pause as the ship again lapsed into silence. No sound to contend with the swish of the bark as she glided through the crisp water—the breeze twanging in the rigging, mumbling a bass accompaniment in the hollow of the sails.

The sea was like oiled lead, the dawn mist lightly drifting, the sky now an unbroken blue-gray. Any sea-

man could sense wind and squalls somewhere off to the south. Clouds of uneasy seafowl were wheeling about as though in warning, and Jess noted the sinister nimbus bank whose sudden appearance off the African coast always presaged a storm of great violence.

Then they all saw her at once—the oncoming ship—and a low, unconscious gasp ran through the *Bunyan*'s crew.

The dim object enveloped by the opaque moon-struck vapors was the outline of a ship, right enough, but there was something queer about her, something ghastly strange or wrong. She was a ship out of the past. Her design—the high old-fashioned poop especially—denoted that. She had three masts with long yards swung 'thwart ship, but bare of any sails save a few rotting streamers.

Yet, somehow, without a soul on deck to haul on

tack or sheet, the strange ship luffed. She went into stays
and then sluggishly came about on the starboard tack
and slowly forged toward the *Bunyan*.

A thrill of superstitious fear ran icy fingers down
Jess's spine and the hair on his neck tingled.

The spars, cordage, a great part of her bulwarks
were rotted and green with growth. Battered and moldy,
the queer castellated fo'c'sle seemed caved in from
sheer decay and was white with rime. Toward the
high stern everything was covered with sea moss and
the broken, carved woodwork was a roost for row upon
row of solemn white noddies. And what was worse—
what was fearful to see in its ghastly incredibility—
plants and creepers were actually growing out of her.

In the water alongside appeared monster trailing
weeds, and her scarred, moss-grown planks showed
huge barnacles. She was as unhealthy looking as lep-
rosy; a shadowy, antique, forlorn ship—sinister as it
lay there in the red eye of the setting moon.

"A derelict," Starr called from the poop. "Nothing
but a drifting hulk."

"Aye," Ralls said quietly, "but mark her age. She
must date back to the Revolutionary War."

An uncanny silence settled over the crew as they
stared, fascinated, at the decrepit hulk. Then Barnaby
spoke the thought that so many of the superstitious
seamen were secretly thinking.

"Ghost ship."

"Belay that!" Starr called. "That's granny talk."

The *Bunyan* raised the Cape Verde Islands the next

day, and that was the first thing they had seen beyond the plate of sea and the bowl of sky and the derelict in thirty-two days. The second thing they saw was a pod of sperm whales.

The mastheads had had their best eyes bribed by the offer of a golden guinea to the first man who cried "Blows!" And to the common whaleman, who was breaking his back for two or three years to receive his two-hundredth lay of the voyage profits, the guinea had the aspect of an Aztec treasure.

It worked like this:

There were no wages aboard a whaler. Everyone was paid off in lays, on the profit-sharing system. With greasy luck the *Bunyan* would complete her voyage with 2,400 barrels of oil in her hold, worth some sixty shillings the barrel, which was fifteen American dollars. The common seaman received the two-hundredth lay which would be twelve barrels, or one-hundred-eighty dollars. Which, Jess thought, was surely a mighty poor reward for such racking work and harsh treatment and the manifold dangers.

A harpooner, on the other hand, made out almost as well as the captain. Each harpooner received the twentieth lay; ten times the lot of the common seaman. One hundred and twenty barrels, or eighteen hundred dollars. It was even more than the allotment of the three mates who drew the twenty-fifth, thirty-fifth and fifty-fifth lay, respectively.

The captain, of course, received the best lay of all; the one-sixteenth lay, plus a bonus from the owners for a successful voyage.

No wonder that the golden guinea Captain Coffin had offered was such tempting bait to the seamen to keep a sharp eye seaward!

A man named Nehemiah in the foremasthead won the coveted prize. When his call came it was high, joyous and prolonged—Nehemiah nearly cracking his throat that no one should get ahead of him in his claim for the guinea.

"She BLOWS! *B-L-O-W-S*! Sparm whales to larb'rd! A pod of 'em!"

To Jess the sudden cry was the accumulation of all his setaside childhood dreams of adventure, of danger and derring-do. He dropped his holystone, springing from grime-stained knees to bare feet, and plunged into the infectious aura of apprehension and excitement that emanated from his shipmates.

In that tense, brittle moment he was very glad he was aboard the *Bunyan*.

Bare feet slapped on the decks, men shouted about nothing at all, the officers roared inarticulate orders, everybody rushed for the bulwarks, for the shrouds, and Nehemiah continued to cry ecstatically from the masthead.

"There she blows! Blows on the lee quarter!"

"Hard over with the helm!" Starr yelled at the helmsman. "Luff, you scum! Luff!"

From the poopdeck Captain Coffin's thin reedy voice piped orders in near hysteria.

"Man the braces, Mr. Starr! Stand by to wear! Where is my glass? Why won't somebody find me my glass?" And he went *thunk-thunk-thunk* here, there, everywhere on his whalebone-knobbed cane, his crabbed fingers clutching it like talons around a ball of spun yarn.

Jess scrambled up the fore shrouds and stopped ten feet above the deck. Shading his eyes, he looked out over the blue chopping sea. At first he saw nothing except the faint purplish hump of Cape Verdes far off in the southeast. Then he spotted a thin, vaporish glint of spray a long long way off the lee quarter. It hung in the pallid air for a moment, then dissipated as if by magic and was gone.

Was that all, he wondered. Weren't they to see more of the whale than that? He was disappointed.

The old man had finally found his glass and he came thunking along the deck to find an advantageous spot in which to use it. Nobody seemed to pay much attention to him.

"Hanna!" Starr roared. "Get down from them shrouds afore I flay you to ribbons! Look alive, every man jack!"

The mates went after the crew with curses and rope-ends as the ponderous *Bunyan* began to pay off to leeward, driving them to slack away on the lee sheets and braces and hove taut on the windwards.

Jess hauled energetically on the briny lines, working shoulder to shoulder with Barnaby and Tavi. *We'll go after him now*, he thought. *We'll lower away and go out there and fight him. Will I be scared? Will I be killed or maimed like Starr?*

Slowly the *Bunyan* came around and the whale spouts began to haul forward along the larboard beam.

The blunt forefoot bit in and the parings of waves flowed aft along the heeled-down lee rail.

"Masthead there!" Starr called. "How do ye make her?"

A sperm whale is regulated like a clock. Every ten seconds, while it is on the surface, it will send a fountain of steamy vapor through its blowhole.

There was a pause, and a count—eight nine ten—then:

"She blows! Broad off the larboard beam!"

"Steady as she goes!" Starr ordered the helmsman.

Captain Coffin was trying to get an order in edgewise, and finally Starr turned an exasperated face toward him to listen.

"Send the cooper to the masthead, Mr. Starr. And the cook to take the wheel!"

"Aye, sir, I know," the mate said gruffly, and turned away to pass the order.

The *Bunyan* was shorthanded. Her compliment was only twenty-one men: captain, cook, cooper, three mates, three harpooners and twelve seamen before the mast. This meant she could only lower three boats at a time. It was up to the captain and the cook and cooper to manage the ship when the boat crews went out to fight the whales.

A man by the larboard cathead called, "There goes flukes!"

Jess looked ahead and saw the tall fan-shaped tail of the whale swing into the air, pause for a moment as it fluttered gracefully, then go down straight into the sea like a sinking ship going down by the bow, and disappear.

The whale had sounded.

"Now what?" Jess asked Barnaby.

"A full hour he'll stay below, me bucko. 'Tis his nature, do 'ee see? But don't ask me why. Then he'll up again to get himself a spot of air. And losh! We'll be there waiting for him, so we will!"

The mates started choosing their crews. Starr, of course, had first pick and he used his privilege to select the most likely men. Going down the anxious line of seamen and harpooners, he made a canny selection.

"Jekiel Burr, you'll harpoon for me. Barnaby, you tosspot Irishman, you'll take my waist oar. Jehiel Galpin, you take the tub oar."

He paused in front of Jess and looked him up and down as if he were contemplating the purchase of a horse. The fingers of his left hand bit into Jess's shoulder like marlin spikes.

"You're a husky lad, Hanna, and with a generous reach to your arms. You'll be my stroke oar. And—" he added menacingly, "I'll gut ye for dinner if you don't give me a stroke like Satan's whip!"

It meant that he would have to set the pace for the whaleboat and maintain it, but right at that moment Jess was too starryeyed with excitement to care, or to remember that he hated Starr like poison. He grinned.

"Aye, sir," he said.

Starr picked a man named Abiel Cook for the second bow oar.

They gathered along the bulwark on the larboard side. All American whalers were designed with two small, elevated boatdecks spanning the waist. These racks were used to carry the spare boats, which was a very necessary precaution in the whaling industry. A whale could smash or chew up a boat in less time than a masthead could cry *Blows!*

Starr's boat was the bow larboard boat. It was swayed out on the cranes as his crew lined up, ready at the command to pile overboard.

Each boat carried six men: a mate as steersman in the stern, the harpooner in the bows, and four rowers —stroke oar, tub oar, waist oar, second bow oar. The harpooner was required to pull the starboard bow oar until the boat came up on the whale.

While waiting for the sixty minutes to pass, Burr busied himself honing the barbed head of his harpoon, and Starr whetted the heart-shaped point of his eight-foot lance. It was the harpooner's job to secure the whale to the boat with his harpoon, and the mate's job to kill the whale with his lance.

A harpoon never killed a whale. It could only penetrate a short distance through the fatty blubber of the leviathan's tough hide. It was the long slender lance that probed inside the great body and struck the vital organs that told the tale.

A heavy, expectant silence settled over the ship. No one spoke. All eyes watched for the rising mammal. Then from the lookout—which was kept on the knighthead where the bowsprit met the ship—a sharp cry rang out.

"There she white-waters!"

A thick thrash of churned water foamed on the surface and the mighty sperm whale came up with a tall fountain of spray shooting from his blowhole. He was nearly a mile off and he started swimming to wind-ward with slow, lazy sweeps of his massive tail, looking for all the world like a great shapeless shining mound of India rubber.

"Larboard!" Starr roared at the helmsman.

At the order the helmsman luffed sharply to deaden the headway and the old whaler sagged up into the wind, topsails flapping.

"All right, blast your eyes!" Starr bellowed indiscriminately. "A dead whale or a stove boat! *LOWER AWAY!*"

The crew echoed the old whaler warcry—"A dead whale or a stove boat."

All along the larboard the boat falls ran out and the bow boat dropped from the davit heads. Jess scrabbled over the rail and into the dropping boat with the mate, Jekiel the harpooner, Barnaby, Jehiel and Abiel. Jehiel and Abiel slacked off at the davit cleats and the boat met the water with a wet smack and started to rock precariously.

No one seemed conscious of the danger of being smashed against the towering hull of the whaler. Time was all that counted now. Time meant oil and oil meant money and the seamen were in a great hurry to keep their rendezvous with danger; perhaps with death.

For the sperm whale was like no other whale in the sea. Vicious, crafty, vindictive, he seemed to have a mind that was geared to malevolence. He liked to fight back, and the odds were heavy in his favor.

Starr in the stern and Jekiel in the bow, they cast loose. Then Jekiel gave a sharp shove and the bow swung away from the rolling hull of the *Bunyan*. Out went the sweeps and the mate shipped his steering oar astern.

"Give way!" he snarled at them.

Jess dug his bare heels into the planking and laid all of himself into the long hard haul. At that vivid moment he was willing to tear his arms from their sockets to please the glowering mate.

It was hard work—the hardest ever (if Mrs. Folger could see him now!), dragging back on his twelve-foot ash oar. Thank God he didn't have to haul the waist oar—Barnaby's—which was the longest in the boat, a sixteen-foot sweep.

Jess could hear Jehiel's grunted breath right behind him at the tub oar. Jehiel had to contend with the harpoon line tub which was set between his splayed feet.

Each boat contained five oars, a steering oar, a mast and a spirtsail, a keg of water, a keg of biscuits, a lantern, a waterproof match keg, a bailing pail and bucket, a boat spade and ax, a flag or "wheft," and a line tub.

This tub was the most prominent and important part of a whaleboat's gear. Three feet in diameter, it contained 200 fathoms of manila rope which was coiled in a smooth spiral, concentric scroll, layer after layer right up to the rim of the tub, so that the tub looked like a great round golden cheese.

The harpooners were responsible for these tubs and they exerted great care in coiling the lines into them —even going so far as to run one end of the line up the rigging to the masthead to put it through a block and drop it down to the deck, to insure against kinks or knots or any twist or turn.

That was all it took to snatch a man by the arm or leg or neck and whip him overboard when a harpooned whale sounded—just one wrong twist in the tub-line.

The tub was placed on the floorboards just behind the stroke oarsman. The line went aft and wound itself around the loggerhead which was a two-foot high sternpost. Reversing its direction, the line then ran forward between the staggered oarsmen to the bow chock, passed through an eye in the chock and was attached to the butt end of the harpoon. The harpoons (there were two of them, both attached to the line) rested in a forked crotch which protruded over the whaleboat's starboard bow. The mate's three lances were housed in a crotch on the larboard side.

How six men were supposed to manage themselves among all that gear and the deadly harpoon line was more than Jess could imagine. But right at that moment there was no time for reflection upon any subject except rowing.

Starr, crouching over the steering oar, raved at them like a madman.

"*PULL!* Pull like you were pulling yourselves out of the mouth of Hades instead of going into it—*which you are!* Pull till her keel is clear of the water and she walks on the oarblades alone! Pull till your guts squeeze through your bellybuttons! *Pull!*"

They pulled.

"Pull, blast you for sogers! Break something, can't

you? Break the blinking oars if you can't break your backs! Lean and reach and pull! Flukes and flames! Can't you lubbers hear what I say? I said *PULL PULL PULL!*"

At each back drag Jess's head arched upward and he saw the pallid sun and the sharp blue sky around it. His lungs panted like swelling bellows and his muscles leaped and quivered all along his salt-stained arms and the oar seemed to have the heft of a main topsail yard.

And still Starr was not satisfied.

"Pull till your tongues turn to black leather, till your eyes roll red in their sockets!" he harangued them. "Start her, I say! Start her! Rip out the blasted gunnels! Break the blasted oarlocks! Snap the blasted sweeps!"

From the way Starr was carrying on, Jess figured the whale must be at least five miles ahead of them and with never a chance of their catching up to him. He started to turn his head to glance over his shoulder, to see if they were gaining at all.

"No!" Starr exploded. "Don't look, Hanna! I'll stove the head of any man that looks around! Look aft at me! *I'm* your eyes. Pull and start her!"

Jess didn't especially want to look at Starr. The mate was acting like a maniac. He let his eyes go astern. Far back across the chopping water he saw the other two larboard boats struggling away from the tall ship which was now falling off from the wind to fill sails again and stand on, tacking after the three boats in a haphazard manner.

"I said *on me*, Hanna!" Starr roared. "Never mind the ship! She'll still be there after you're all dead and gone and nothing but picked bones on the bottom of the sea. Lay into it, my sons! Snatch and pull and shear the tholepins off! Blast your lubberly souls! Can't you do this one thing for me? Haven't I been like a father to you?"

Jess would have liked to have told him, but this was not the time or place for personalities. It was not what Starr said that mattered, anyhow—it was his manner of saying it. He ruled them with his voice, not his words. The maniacal glint in his flashing eyes seemed to hypnotize them to his will.

Suddenly Jess realized that Starr was deceiving them. They *were* gaining. Because all at once a new sound started to mingle with their labored breathing and with the creaking and muffled thump of the oars —a great sharp sucking in and a slow expelling of a ton of air, as if the soul of the sea were snoring in its briny sleep.

They must be drawing very close to the whale now.

Starr, leaning against the steering oar and clutching the haft in the curve of his hook, hissed at them urgently.

"On me! On me! Your eyes on me, else I'll crown ye with the boat spade!"

He gave a pull on the steering oar and sheered the boat a little to larboard and the chop went out of the wash from their oars on the starboard.

We must be practically against him! Jess thought. He glanced at Starr, saw the mate crouching and staring straight ahead, and decided he must risk one quick look. He rolled his head and eyes to starboard.

A great slick black hill sprawled before them, so close it did something to Jess's heart—a catch and miss. He had a flickering impression in the corner of his eye of a peculiar slithering motion just barely beneath the surface. Whale flukes!

Abruptly, Starr's bellowing harangue terminated.

"Silence all!" he whispered to the five men who had not once said a word since they had gone over the *Bunyan*'s side.

"One word will gally the whale and he'll off to soundings! Quiet now . . . wait . . . wait for it . . . but stand by to pull like possessed demons when I give the word." His eyes glittered fanatically as he crouched above Jess in the sternsheets.

"Stand up, Jekiel," he hissed.

Jekiel Burr quietly shipped his oar and rose to his feet, turned and picked up the first long harpoon and raised it over his right shoulder, taking aim. He braced his left leg in the knee-rest cleat in the bow.

Jess snapped his eyes around, looked at the tub just behind his thwart, at the line leading from it to the loggerhead and then forward past his right shoulder to the bow chock and the harpoon. In a moment now that line would start to life, would sing, and the whaleboat would be as tightly drawn together as an archer's bow.

Any foul turn, he thought apprehensively, *can whip about a man and snap him right from the boat. Pull him down deep in the sea.* He swallowed and edged an inch outboard on the thwart, trying to put a little space between himself and that deadly line.

Starr was speaking again, and his voice was like a mother's whisper of love.

"Oh Lord, it's beautiful! *Beautiful.* Jekiel—if you love me, Jekiel—"

Abruptly he jammed the steering oar to larboard, sheering the boat spang toward the whale-hill, his face contorted in total frenzy, all caution gone.

"PULL ALL! Beach me on yon hump! *Beach me,* blast you!"

Jess's rump left the thwart as he lunged back on his oar. The boat leaped ahead, jolted, then canted up slightly in the bow as if it had gone aground.

"Give it to him, Jekiel!" Starr screamed.

"Yah!" Jekiel cried, and they all heard the *tunk* of the harpoon spitting the blubber.

Jess swung his head around and saw the iron sink home to the hitches, the wooden shaft protruding from the shiny black skin and quivering spastically—and saw Jekiel snatch up the second iron, swing it high and plunge it into the huge gleaming hump.

Immediately everything was chaos.

Alongside, the hill of whale became an earthquake, rolling violently sideways, and a wall of green-white water built up and washed the boat to a high precarious platform. Then they slid down, tumbling and clutching and all hands shouting meaningless sound, with the tub-line whirring overhead.

Something black, gigantic and reaching came out of the shattered sea and arched into the sky—forty feet of it. The boat was spinning crazily in a wild trough underneath.

"She flukes!"

Jess looked up. It was the massive black tail that stood high above them, draining silver-white water, cutting out the sun and casting a shadow over them with its flukes like a dark omen. In a moment, a split moment, that tail would descend upon them like a falling roof.

Everything inside Jess sagged into limbo. He was too terrified to move a muscle. His mouth dropped open, gaping upward.

"*STERN ALL!*" Starr bellowed. "Stern for your lives!"

Jess couldn't see that they had a chance in the world to backwater the boat clear of the descending flukes. The roof was already falling in.

He didn't know that he was making a decision. What he did was without physical effort, without conscious direction of his will. He simply reacted on the instinct of self-preservation.

He scrambled up from the floorboards and jumped overboard.

5. I Can't Run Away From It

THERE WAS a reverberant thump somewhere in the water, muted by his pressured ears. He couldn't see a thing. The water was as opaque as green-tinted milk-glass. He felt something, though—a rushing passage in the water nearby, and he felt a down drag. He started clawing for the surface with a touch of panic.

He couldn't understand when he came to the surface why he was alone. He looked around for the bobbing heads of his shipmates, for the pieces of boat wreckage, but he saw nothing.

Were they crushed to death? he wondered breakly. *Didn't they jump in time?*

Then he heard a distant shout behind him. He finned himself about and, rising sharply on the crest of an oily swell, he saw Starr's boat skimming off across the sea. The harpooned whale was taking the mate for a "Nantucket sleigh ride."

Jess was alone in the water. The others hadn't jumped.

The third mate's boat had caught a breeze and came heeling by with its lugsail fat and proud. Gant was acting as Starr's escort, or loose boat. None of the third mate's crew paid the slightest attention to Jess treading forlornly in the water, though he raised a hand to them and called on Gant.

"Mr. Gant! Here! Over here!"

Gant glanced in his direction and gave a quick, humorless grin. Then he turned his head forward and yelled at his crew.

"Mind the trim, you lubbers! We're spilling wind!"

Jess watched them going after Starr's runaway boat as he rose and fell with the roll of the water and he couldn't understand.

Didn't they see me? he wondered. *Couldn't they hear me?*

The third boat was coming on. Mr. Ralls's boat. Jess, starting to fag out now, raised his hand again and waved frantically. Then he sagged back in the water. They had seen him and were coming for him.

The bow of the boat clove toward him. Ralls leaned on his steering oar and sheered off the head, and ordered, "Belay oars."

Jess swam over to the idle boat and the stroke oarsman poked out his sweep to Jess so that he could haul himself up the shaft to the gunwale. None of them offered a hand, none of them spoke to him.

It surprised him. He had expected them to josh him unmercifully about his narrow escape, as was the natural way with all rough-humored seamen. But they didn't even look at him.

Jess hoisted himself over the side abaft the stroke-oar thwart and slumped on the boards in a wringing-wet heap, gasping and spewing water. When his breath was recovered he grinned ruefully and tried to make a joke of it himself.

"Well, surely didn't know it would be like *that*," he said. "Not like a hurricane with a twister thrown in!"

The stroke oar looked at him, a flat cold study.

"Give way," Ralls ordered quietly.

Jess pulled his eyes from the blank-faced stroke oar and looked up at Ralls.

"What's wrong?" he asked anxiously. "Was somebody killed?"

"No!" the harpooner called from the bows, his face a tight angry mask. "Nobody was killed—no thanks *to you!*"

"Belay that!" Ralls said. "Mind your oar—and your own business."

Jess blinked at the second mate.

"What is it, sir?" he asked. "I don't understand."

Ralls removed his pipe from his mouth and looked at it, top and bottom, as though he saw something strange in it. He spoke in a toneless voice.

"It doesn't do any good to jump when a whale raises his flukes over a boat. Because eight times out of ten he'll still get you—in the boat or in the water.

"It's the duty of every man to stick to his station on his sweep, to backwater and get the boat clear of the flukes. *You* didn't stick. That left only three oarsmen to try to save the boat, the mate, the harpooner and themselves. They might all have been killed—because you jumped."

Jess had a queer, empty look on his face as he stared down at his oar-blistered hands. A coppery taste came into his mouth, but he had no saliva left to spit it out.

"I didn't know," he said quietly. "I didn't understand. I thought it was the only thing left to do. I thought they were all doing it."

His head came up and his eyes glared.

"*I didn't know,* Mr. Ralls!" he nearly yelled. "Nobody told me!"

Ralls returned the pipe to his mouth and slanted his eyes at the sea. Far off in the east Starr's whale was wallowing fin-up on the surface. Dead.

Starr was in an icy rage when he reached the *Bunyan*'s deck. He glared from right to left at the mute seamen in the waist.

"Where's that Jumping Jack?" he demanded. "Where's Hanna hiding?"

Jess stepped out, the queer coppery taste in his mouth again.

"I'm not hiding," he said.

"Ain't you?" the mate jeered. "Well, you'll soon wish you were. I'll teach you what it means to jump from a boat of mine!"

He stalked toward Jess, bunching his burly shoulders.

"Listen," Jess said, "you can't blame a man for an innocent mistake, can you? I didn't know any better! I thought it was the only sensible thing to do."

"Aye," Starr sneered, "and now I'm going to learn you better in the only sensible way there is!"

He rushed Jess with a viciousness that was momentarily overwhelming. Jess fought back—tried to—but he was no match for the giant mate, or for that hook. His fists seemed to bounce off Starr's elbows, while Starr's blows thudded home to his heart and belly. The hook caught in his belt and held him. A knee came up and rammed him in the groin. Jess gasped in pain, wrapped his arms around the mate and hung on, trying to side-punch. A fist drummed on his kidney, and he heard a voice a long way off jeering.

"I knew you didn't have it in you from the first, my son. I knew you was all heft and no guts!"

A bombshell of hatred exploded in Jess's mind. He gathered together all his strength and flung Starr from him—the hook snapping his belt in two.

The mate spun across the deck, crashed into Nehemiah, who went down in a tangled heap with him and lay still as Starr bounded to his feet, kicked the prostrate Nehemiah in an orgy of rage and started hulking toward Jess, raising his hook.

"Now," he hissed, "I'm going to feed you steel, Jumping Jack!"

"I'll not have it, Mr. Starr!" a reedy voice spoke.

Jess's eyes cleared. The speaker, he saw, was Captain Coffin, who stood between him and Starr with a cocked boarding pistol in his gnarled hand.

The waist swarmed like a hive as seamen and officers trundled out of the line of fire of that trembling pistol in the old man's shaky hand.

"A lashing I'll abide," the captain said in his cackle voice. "But I'll have no killings aboard my ship! We need the men."

"Gut me for a cod!" Starr raged. "Did I say I'd kill him? I only meant *to open him!* But when it comes to killing—I've that right, and well ye know it. He hit me—and that's mutiny!"

A gleam of mad humor came into Starr's icy eyes.

"But I won't kill him. Oh no. That would be too easy. I'm going to save him for better things." Starr looked at the old man.

"That suit you, Captain?" he asked.

The captain stood there, suddenly slack, only his cane holding him up—like a man going slowly into a dream. The emotional fire charred out in his sick eyes.

"Whatever you say, Mr. Starr," he mumbled. "I leave the crew in your hands. Only remember that we need every hand . . ." His voice trailed off and so did he, dragging himself aft to his cabin.

Starr watched him go. Then he swung back to Jess.

"Hanna," he said in a low voice, "I've beat you and hazed you for four weeks. But now I see that's the wrong way to break you down. Well—from now on, my son, we'll try a different tack."

He became the trypot boy, and that was all Starr would let him be. Seventeen years of growing up to

that one moment before he leaped out of the boat—
and after it the crew put their backs to him, referred
to him among themselves as the "Jumping Jack" and
pretended he no longer existed.

And he was doomed to live with them in that 300-
ton whaler for two more years.

It was done on Starr's order of course. Captain Coffin, who had been resurrected from some whaleman's
boneyard by Mr. Munro, was so old and feeble he
was now nearly infirm. He was a figurehead skipper.
It was Starr's iron will that held the *Bunyan* afloat
and in business.

When a whale or a pod was sighted, Starr's standing order was:

"Keep that Jumping Jack clear of the boats."

And the boats would lower and go off to fight the
whales—and Jess would be left aboard the *Bunyan*
with the senile captain, the fat cook and the crotchety
cooper.

He never said anything about it. There was nothing
to say; no one to say it to. He created a little island of
silence. Where he went a hush followed—talk ceased,
laughter broke short, eyes turned to the sea or to the
palm-and-fid work with exaggerated concentration,
and Jess passed on alone.

It was a freeze-out; and though some of them—like
Barnaby or Pie-face—felt sorry for him and were
tempted to speak to him, they were too afraid of the
brutal mate to break his law. So Jess dwelt in loneliness, like a deaf-mute in a crowd.

After a whale was killed it was lashed to the *Bun-*

yan's hull and the cutting-in began. The seamen swayed cutting stages over the side and the mates went to work on the dead leviathan with their flensing spades, cutting into the fatty layer of blubber.

The dead whale was rigged head to stern, tail to bow with a chain-loop around his tail and cinched tight to his flukes. It was the harpooners' job to fight off the voracious sharks with the razor-sharp boat spades.

These sharks were so ferocious, especially in southern waters, that they would come at a dead whale in droves—knifing in and finning over and snapping out a watermelon-sized bite of blubber, and veering off to gulp down their mouthful, and then gliding on around to dart in and make another strike.

The harpooners struck at their heads, backs, bellies, anything that showed; and it was rather weird to watch a gut-split shark gobble at a dead whale while his own entrails strung out in the water, with still another shark eating his escaping innards. And sometimes a gutted shark would be so mad with the bloodlust that he would wobble off in a C-shape snapping at, and swallowing, his own unraveling intestines.

Once Jekiel and another harpooner named Bent managed to catch a blue shark on a hook and line and they hauled the jerking, tail-slapping fish on deck.

Starr inserted a stake sharpened on both ends between the shark's wide-open jaws and dumped the luckless thing back in the sea. With that stake in its stretched mouth, the shark would either drown itself or starve to death, or find itself defenseless against the attack of other sharks. Starr thought it was a great joke.

After the first cutting-in stage, huge blankets of blubber were unrolled from the whale's carcass and hoisted inboard by block and tackle, then lowered into the hatch of the blubber room just below the trypots.

This was Jess's department.

Jammed into the stinking little room, squeezing himself in as best he could between the greasy masses of fat, he would cut the blubber up into "horse pieces" —each piece about eighteen inches by six inches.

It was the most ghastly job imaginable. He became totally saturated with oil, as if he had been dipped into a tank of it. The ship rolled—Jess fell: every fall upon blubber blankets running with oil. He waded in oil up to his ankles. The fat, oozing mattresses of blubber pressed in on him. There was no air to breathe. The ship rocked and pitched. His very pores squeegeed oil.

When this amusing chore was completed, Starr had him fetched on deck and put him to the task of mincing the horse pieces. Once the blubber was minced it was dumped into great tubs, and from the tubs it went to the tryworks.

The tryworks were two enormous pots set in a brick frame amidships, under the forward boatrack. Under each pot was a kiln that needed constant feeding and ate only cast-off chunks of blubber. At one side of the tryworks was a wooden hopper containing the raw minced blubber. At the other end was a copper cistern into which the prepared oil was bailed to cool.

It was there that Jess toiled, with the red mouths of the two furnaces scolding at him for more fuel, with the boiling oil sloshing and exploding and the gray smoke—greasy and sickening—kicking about sluggishly underfoot.

He stuck at it grimly, week after week, agleam with whale oil and sweat, half blinded and gasping from smoke; speaking to no one and trying to pretend he didn't notice his shipmates, who were pretending not to notice him.

The *Bunyan* pounded south, and then southeast. Off the Cape of Good Hope she struck a wet easter that kept her clawing offshore for its duration, but she sighted the lighthouse of Cape Agulhas the morning of her seventy-third day out of New Bedford, and the next day she stood in past a bluff headland to come to anchor about midafternoon in Mossel Bay, which stood at the forefoot of the great continent of Africa.

Starr himself had conned the ship to her berth, but he showed no signs of wanting to go ashore. He and Ralls studied the Dutch fort and the wharves of the shoddy little town massed around the land battlements of Africa's mountains through a spyglass.

"I don't trust all them heathens," Starr said. "We'll let them come out to us."

They came soon enough—the Dutch first, to see what they could sell to the whaler; then the Negroes in their longboats (once their Dutch masters had learned that the *Bunyan* needed water), and swarmed alongside and started rigging the hauls to the bulky hogsheads, chattering all the while like schoolboys the instant their owner's back was turned.

Jess could sympathize with them and appreciate the exuberance they showed over their so-called holiday. He felt like a slave himself.

Fresh water was a precious commodity aboard a whaler, and Starr made a point of this fact. A great scuttlebutt was kept by the cabin door in the stern, and it was to this butt that every seaman had to go to get himself a drink.

Only one balerful per man was allowed. No water could be carried away. The crew was required to wash themselves and their clothes in seawater—which simply could not be done. If a man tried to wash in cold saltwater he quickly found himself covered with a fine green slime; and his clothes—always greasy with oil—came out the same way.

The *Bunyan* weathered the Cape of Good Hope and stood eastward into the trades. And it was as though she were inexorably running into a great sea of unavoidable bad luck . . . .

In the Agulhas Current they lost three pods of whales in as many days. Off Madagascar Ralls's harpooner was pounded to pulp under the smashing flukes of a sperm whale and whisked into eternity without a cry. And two days later Starr's new stroke oar, 'Lisha Nook, lost a foot in a giant spermaceti's rising jaws —while his horrified shipmates, swimming right below him in the tangled wreckage of their boat, watched.

"Why doesn't Starr blame it on me?" Jess said bitterly to Ralls that night as they shared a watch. The second mate was the only man aboard the *Bunyan* who was not afraid to talk to him. "After all, 'Lisha took my place."

Ralls, removing his pipe, inspecting it for flaws, nodded.

"He does," he said. "He thinks it *should* have been you. 'Lisha is one of Starr's toadies, and he was planning on making him my new harpooner. Now I'm to receive Nehemiah."

Ralls was pensive for a moment, thinking. Then he said:

"Yes, I think Starr is very disappointed that it wasn't you who lost a foot. I really believe he would like to see you a cripple."

Then a northwester overtook them and the old spouter drove before its blasts with shortened canvas and battened hatches. For five days it hounded them, piling up the waves to mountainous proportions; and that cost them a man along with a starboard boat— both swept overboard at night and never seen again.

After that there was another stove boat and then a whaleman with stove ribs off Reunion Island. And finally there came the murmurings among the crew of a "Joner" being aboard.

It was the inevitable conclusion. Superstition has always been a tradition of the sea. Now the *Bunyan* was out of luck and there had to be a reason for it. She had lost three whale pods, three boats, two men, and two other men were in sickbay. The crew needed a scapegoat to blame their trouble on. A Jonah seemed the obvious answer.

The day Ralls heard of the "Joner" rumor he tucked

his pipe out of sight in his watch coat, gathered the
crew together in the waist and talked to them like a
mild-mannered schoolmaster reprimanding a class of
rowdy children.

"Stop it," he said to them in his quiet way. "Granny
talk only breeds fear, and fear is the father of trouble.
What do you expect when you try to make a pincushion
of a whale? There's always a stove boat and a drowned
man, and a storm always leaves its mark. Jonah? Your
Jonah is your own superstition. We'll have no more of
such talk."

Jess thanked the second mate that night under the
after boatrack.

"I know who they had in mind when they talked of
a Jonah," he said grimly. "If they had their way
they'd probably ship me overboard."

"You can't really blame them," Ralls said. "They're
afraid of our run of bad luck and they're afraid of
Starr. If he keeps driving them this way, they'll turn
on us. Or turn on each other.

"And for that matter," he added, "you're not doing
yourself any good by staying with us. Starr will never
let you taste blood now. You'll be the trypot boy for
the next two years. You see? He thinks this is the way
to break your spirit."

Jess nodded moodily. "And he just might be right.
I'd rather fight him and a whale both than go on like
this."

"Look here," Ralls said. "The next time we speak
another whaler—why don't you ship over to it? You'd
go with a clean slate."

Jess shook his head doggedly. "No. For one thing, Starr would never let me go. For another—I wouldn't go if I had the chance."

"Why?" Ralls looked mildly amazed.

"Because I made a mistake and I haven't been given the chance to make up for it," Jess said. "I can't run away from it—couldn't live with it. And I can't let Starr get the best of me."

He turned to Ralls. "Look"—and held out his arms, long, muscular, gleaming like ivory in the moonlight —"look what the tryworks have done for me. I think I can outrow any man aboard this ship, and would, too, if it would prove anything to them."

"It wouldn't."

"But don't you see?" Jess appealed. "I'd make the best stroke oar of all. And I wouldn't jump. I wouldn't, Mr. Ralls—no matter what happened to the boat. Help me, can't you? Help me convince the captain I should be put back in the boats. He's got the power to go over Starr's orders."

Ralls slapped the bowl of his pipe into his palm and squinted at the little black lump of dottle.

"I've already tried that," he said. "I brought it up with him this evening."

"And?"

"Maybe you'd better try to jump ship if you get the chance, Hanna. Captain Coffin has given Starr full authority over the crew."

6. A Mean Creature Is An Ironed Spermaceti

THE OLD spouter hammered along through short tumbling seas, following in the wake of a whale vein.

On the days and nights when there had been a kill, Jess would work in the blubber room and at the trypots. When they didn't bring him blubber, Starr would have him inside the pots scouring them with soapstone.

But he never complained; would never say anything to the mate except, "Aye aye, sir."

The need for atonement, and the desire to beat Starr at his own game, became an obsession with him. His bunk was a blanket mangle of restless frustration. He would toss out of it at any hour of night and go topside to prowl the deck, to stare at the darkly rolling sea. He ate his food squatting off alone, not watching what he was eating, masticating and swallowing from habit and not from hunger. He scoured and bailed, fed blubber to fire and sweated through smoke that was like hot rancid butter.

And sometimes he would be found standing in the waist doing nothing—standing with his fists clenched, staring down at the holystoned deck.

One day they "spoke" another whaler. As was the custom, both ships luffed sharply and came up in the wind to deaden their headway. With the topsails flapping idly overhead, Starr went over the side to go have a gam with the other spouter.

The *Bunyan*'s crew watched Jess to see what he would do or say. He did nothing. He stared at the distant whaler for a moment, then turned from the bulwark and went below. Mr. Gant's grating laugh and mocking words followed him down the companion.

"Told you so! He's gutless. Afraid to join another ship where he'd be expected to taste blood."

Jess knew it would do no good to defend himself. All he could do was wait for his chance to show Starr and the rest of them that he was as much a man as any seaman aboard the *Bunyan*. He waited a full three months and then felt he could wait no longer. The decision came to him one night when he was standing alone on deck.

He was ready to beg, if need be, to bring himself back to man size. He went below to the captain's cabin.

"Aye?" Captain Coffin squeaked at Jess's knock. "Come!"

Jess opened the door and stepped into the cabin—the forbidden place for seamen. It was roomy, clean and airy, bright with moonlight from the windows in the stern, as tidy as a minister's study.

The old man was padding about in the moony dark in his slippers and nightshirt, shuffling and pausing as though not quite certain where he was going next.

"Why is the lantern out?" he mumbled fretfully. "Why doesn't anybody ever take care of anything aboard this ship?"

He suddenly seemed to recall Jess's presence.

"Yes? Yes?" his reedy voice piped. "What now? Who are you?"

"Jess Hanna, sir. I've come to ask you to put me in one—"

"Who? Who? Jess Who?" the old man scuffled around the table, peering and blinking in the shadowy light at Jess.

"Hanna?" he mumbled. "Hanna? Oh! You're the one they call the Jumping Jack, ain't you? Yes, yes, that's who you be. Jumping Jack! *He he he!*"

His cackling seemed to lead his mind astray. He bumped against the table and stared at it vacuously, as though surprised to find it there. "Jumping Jack," he murmured vaguely. "Aye."

"Sir," Jess said, "it was a mistake. It was my first time in a boat and I didn't know better. I'd never jump again. I want another chance, sir. I want to be put in a boat again. I thought maybe you—"

The old man pushed at the table, but it wouldn't go away.

"Starr," he said abruptly. "Starr handles the boats.

See the mate. Aye, see the mate about the boats, he handles 'em. I'm not feeling well . . . no, not very well, thankee."

He started hobbling aft around the table, confusedly, as if wondering why the pesky thing wouldn't get out of his way. Jess went after him, holding out a hand in a gesture of helplessness.

"The mate won't let me near the boats, sir. I thought you could help me. You're the—I mean—"

The old man approached his berth like a rudderless derelict drifting onto a lee shore. His brittle fingers fumbled across the top blanket as though searching.

"My Bible is missing," he muttered childishly. "Someone took my Bible; can't find it anywhere. I told Starr; told him it was missing. Said he'd find it for me, but—"

He hauled himself over the berthboard, mumbling and chuffing, and lay down like a scuttled ship settling on the bottom stern first.

Jess looked at the old man and touched his shoulder in supplication. Captain Coffin stared at the beam overhead.

"A man shouldn't be at sea without his Bible," he said drowsily. "You remember that, lad. My wife gave me mine—forty years ago, I think it was. Starr said he'd find it . . ."

Jess let his hand drop. He nodded heavily.

"Aye, sir," he said quietly. "He'll find it for you."

He walked out of the cabin, closing the door softly behind him. He met Starr in the companionway.

In the oily light cast by the companion lamp, the mate's face looked like beach coral grained with salt, and his eyes had the menacing stare of two long toms before they broadside.

"What're you sogering about down here for, Jumping Jack?"

The mate was the one man in the world with whom Jess did not want to plead. Yet he was the only man who could help him. He held on to Starr's hostile gaze, which was more than most aboard the *Bunyan* could do.

"I want another chance," he said tersely. "I—"

"Been whining to the old man, eh?" Starr snarled.

Jess ignored the insult. "I want back in the boats. I give you my word I won't jump again. I'll give you more than that for a second chance. I'll ask you for it in front of the entire crew, if you'll say yes."

"Would you, Jumping Jack?" Starr grinned a tight, fierce grin. "Would you crawl? Aye, I think you would. Beginning to break, ain't you?" He tapped Jess's chest with his hook.

"Remember the day in that barn when you mocked the whaling industry? Remember when you sneered at George Starr, eh? And what you said about the stinking trypots belonging to somebody with a strong back and a weak mind, eh?" He snorted a harsh laugh.

"Well, now you've got it, my son, and you're going to keep it till you go mad and throw yourself overboard."

He pushed his weathered lump of face close to Jess, his eyes sparkling like two crumbs of glass in the lamplight. And again Jess wondered if Starr was unbalanced.

"You won't be the first, ye know," Starr said in a low, fierce voice. "I've done it to other men—better men than you. And ye won't be the last. Aye, you'll crawl afore I'm done with you! Now sheer off!"

Starr shouldered by him, clumping on down the stairs.

Frustrated and furious by the impotency Starr had imposed on him, Jess shouted after him.

"I'll never leave this ship! You hear me, Starr? Never! I'll stay till you crawl to *me!*"

For three days they chased a whale pod off of the Chagos. During those three days they fought two decisive battles—both in favor of the whales. The first leviathan victory only cost them a boat; the second took the life of one of Gant's oarsmen—crushed like an egg by flukes when a sperm whale sounded.

The *Bunyan* was still keeping her rendezvous with bad luck.

Jess was standing the wheel on the third night and heard Starr and Ralls through the skylight. They were arguing below in the cuddy.

"I said no and I'll stand by that." Starr's voice, flat and uncompromising. "I think you know me, Mr. Ralls."

"But we're shorthanded!" Ralls—close to anger. "Three men dead and 'Lisha still in sickbay. And the old man—well—"

"Then we'll sail short! Hanna stays where he is."

"At least put in at Ceylon. We'll try to replenish the crew. There's always seamen on the beach there."

"What? Leave this pod without one kill? I'd rather cut off my other hand. One of those bulls is worth a hundred and fifty barrels of oil if he's worth a drop! No—we won't change course."

"I don't understand you, Starr. You act as if you wanted the crew killed off."

"That's what whalemen are for, mister. Don't tell me my business!"

"You're a stubborn fool, Starr."

"And you a weak one, mister. Weak enough to let that Jumping Jack's whining turn your head."

"He doesn't whine. He waits."

"Does he? Then let me tell you, mister, just how long he's going to wait . . ."

Jess was glad when he was relieved at the wheel. He didn't want to hear more. He went forward through the cold glow of the horned moon which cocked over him like a devil's cap.

Each day now Jess would stand by the bulwark and stare at Starr as the boats were lowered. And each day Starr would scowl back and go over the rail without a word. And this day was the same—the look, the scowl, and then the mate was overboard and shouting orders from his boat.

But something happened with Ralls's boat. Thomas Pickering, Ralls's stroke oar, was slacking off on the davit cleat and he missed his footing and took a fall into the lowering whaleboat.

"Me elbone!" he cried. "Cracked me giddy elbone!"

Ralls said something profoundly dark and ordered Pickering back aboard the whaler. With an expression of harassment on his somber face, he looked up at the bulwark.

Jess stared down at him, making an invisible bridge between them with his appeal.

A second chance. Give me a second chance. I won't jump.

"Take stroke oar, Hanna!" Ralls called.

Jess piled over the side.

There had been a shake-up among the boat crews since Jess had last gone overboard. Nehemiah was now Ralls's harpooner, Tavi was the second bow oar, Pie-face the waist oar, and Barnaby the tub oar. Ralls shoved the boat away from the side of the whaler, giving it a sharp sheer out, and ordered:

"Give way, and lively!"

Jess braced his feet and leaned into the long pull. He rowed his heart out, laying his body nearly horizontal on every stroke, the muscles in his arms and shoulders and back standing out like tenuous serpents.

Ralls, crouched in the sternsheets with the steering oar, his pipe clenched in his bared teeth, spoke to them with a fierce intensity, giving them a beat in a sort of rhythmic chant.

"Send! . . . Send! . . . Send-her-out-of-the-water, my buckos! Break-the-oars-in-two but send . . . Send . . . Break the-tholepins-if-you'd-rather and send! . . . Send! . . . Tear-out-the gunnels-if-you-must and send!"

Jess, at the stroke oar, made Ralls increase the pace

of his litany; and within minutes his shipmates were sucking and blowing as though strangling in their death throe.

"Drop—drop the giddy stroke, ye blasted Jumping Jack!" they gasped at him.

He ignored them and gritted his teeth in a ghastly grin at Ralls, and slowly the second mate's boat began to crawl up with Starr's. The mate glanced back, looked again, then roared.

"Ralls! Who's that stroke oar? Is that Hanna in there? Why, blast your eyes, mister! I'll break you for that!"

Ralls pulled his pipe from his mouth and grinned across the surging water at Starr.

"Could it wait till after I've made my kill?" he called.

Starr looked ahead as though plotting Ralls's intended course. His eyes were slightly wild.

"Ralls!" he bellowed. "That's *my* kill! You hear me?"

Ralls waved his pipe. "Come help us with it!" he offered. And to his crew, "Send! . . . Send! . . . Send-me-from-the-water-like-a-gull!"

Gradually their boat hauled ahead of the mate's laboring boat, leaving Starr's breeze-diminished oaths and threats behind. Ralls stared fixedly ahead, his eyes bright and clean and young with the promise of combat in them. He lifted his left hand and held it palm flat in the air, ordering the oarsmen to center their eyes on it.

"He rises . . . rises . . ." he whispered. "The biggest

bull in all creation! Over one hundred and fifty barrels of sperm in him, else my mother raised a farmer!"

Jess heard the gurgling wash of a great body and the deep gusty breathing, in-out-in-out, like a blacksmith's bellows. It was indeed a monster of the species. Seventy-five foot, the harpooner judged. Jess didn't look. He kept his eyes riveted on Ralls's suspended hand.

"She blows!" Ralls hissed, "Easy—easy now—wait for it. Nehemiah, stand up!"

Jess watched Ralls's hand. He could hear the wheezing and snorfling of the great bull close by and the minor clattering of the harpooner's preparations as he boated his oar and turned to pick up a harpoon.

Abruptly Ralls's hand flashed down and he jammed the steering oar hard to larboard, shooting the sending whaleboat sharply to starboard.

"*SEND!* Strike, Nehemiah!"

The boat literally leaped forward. Again there was the jolt of the bow and whir of the line as the harpoon darted outboard and landed in the bull's hump with a thump. The whale let out a breathy sound of shock and started to writhe sideways, elevating his enormous flukes in fury.

Then the seaquake exploded under them.

A great foamy whale-made swell rolled up and the boat canted crazily, stern high, and slid down the face of the watery wall like a scared cat. Jess caught a whirling glimpse of Starr's boat plowing into the fray, Jekiel

Burr standing tall in the bows with his harpoon high over his head in both hands.

Then Ralls's boat hit the bottom of the trough and was nearly half buried in a white smother of foam.

"Stern all!" Ralls roared. "Stern for your lives! She flukes!"

Jess lunged forward, digging frantically at the yeasty foam with his oarblade, trying to find solid water to give the blade purchase—but there didn't seem to be any, and no two oarsmen were together in their stroke and the boat skittered to starboard in a wild oblique.

He didn't look up at the tremendous flukes he knew were hanging over his head; he was too busy fighting the careening boat with a singlemindedness of purpose that was like a maniacal fury.

The wounded whale sounded and the waving flukes slammed between the two boats with a rush of air and a crash of glassy water. Someone was screaming something. Jess looked around. It was Starr's exuberant harpooner, Jekiel Burr.

"Got him on both sides! I got an iron in his starboard!"

They sagged on the oars, gasping, looked at each other vacantly, and gawked overboard at a turbulent smear of scarlet froth on the moving water. Ralls looked at Jess, then across the watery breach to Starr, as if to say, *He's still here. He didn't jump.*

Starr seemed to interpret the look correctly. His granitelike face assumed a cryptic expression.

"It ain't over with yet, mister!" he called.

Jess thought it was, or nearly so—but he didn't

know about sperm whales. He relaxed and looked at his raw palms. The unbroken blisters looked like translucent pearls. They stung like sin. But he smiled to himself. In less than an hour the bull would surface and they would go after him and drive the lance into his heart. Then he would be a whaleman who had tasted blood—and Starr could go stick his head in a greasy trypot!

But the crews of both boats were fidgety. They kept biting their salty lips and glancing apprehensively at the water. Nehemiah called aft to Ralls.

"It might be a near thing, Mr. Mate. He's a fighting whale. I seen old iron in him."

Ralls nodded and said, "Way enough," which was the order to boat oars. Then the second mate and the harpooner changed fore and aft positions. It was not an easy task in the crowded boat, with that wicked harpoon line whirring between the oarsmen, and Jess was darned if he could see any sense in the maneuver. It was dangerous and unnecessary. If a harpooner was good enough to put an iron in a whale, he should also be qualified to lance the leviathan when it returned to the surface.

But no; whaling tradition decreed that the mate must always make the kill. The boat bobbing about like a cockleshell, Ralls and Nehemiah—stepping around the tub (the line leaping from the tub like a striking cobra) and over the thwarts and the hafts of the boated oars and around the hunched oarsmen, stumbling over the mast and rolled lugsail, and over the water keg and biscuit keg and match keg and the

lantern and bailer and boatspade and all the rest—
somehow managed to switch positions without anyone
falling overboard or becoming entangled in the flying
line.

"What's Nehemiah mean about a fighting whale?"
Jess asked Barnaby.

"Means he's an old hand, matey. He's been harpooned afore, and got away to tell the tale. When he
comes up now, he'll be after looking for uz, so he
will!"

The running line was now nearly three-quarters out.
If it didn't stop soon, the sounding whale would take
the entire line down with him. Jess looked at the eye
splice in the free end of the warp. It stood out of the
tub like a rattler's horny spur tail.

At least, he thought, *he can't drag us under with
him*.

Suddenly the line stopped its whir and Nehemiah,
wearing canvas pads on his hands to protect his palms,
grabbed it and took two turns with the line about the
loggerhead. Ralls carefully tested the strain on the
line by pressing his leg against it.

"She's slack! Heave in lively!"

With both hands Barnaby started hauling in the line
fist over fist, and Jess coiled the slack as best he was
able in the sternsheets. It was coming in too fast to try
to recoil it in the tub. The wet manila splattered spray
over everything and everybody. The whale was evidently rising rapidly.

They were all watching the water now, silent and

tense, as Barnaby heaved and heaved and Jess coiled loop after loop. Suddenly Starr straightened up, his features jerking out of whack.

"By the great anchor, Ralls! He's under you! *Stern, man!*"

Jess saw the black gleam of a shimmering shape materializing under their boat. He opened his mouth, wrapping his hands hard about the oar handle—but there simply wasn't enough time to backwater.

A mountainous black mass reared out of the sea, kicking the starboard oars high into the air like so many jackstraws. It was the whale's blunt snout and it kept coming, coming—and the long narrow underjaw lined with twenty-eight spikelike teeth slid under the hull to scoop the whaleboat out of the water.

Nothing made sense to Jess. Everything was screaming and smashing. His equilibrium was gone. He was only conscious of a gigantic lifting under him. Men were jumping, diving, tumbling into the sea willy-nilly. Only one repeated word had meaning:

"Jump! Jump! Jump!"

But he wouldn't. He thrashed about desperately amidships, coming up in a trembling half-crouch, and looked straight into the sperm whale's cavernous maw!

It rose sheer above him and around him, and for a suspended moment he saw the deep pits in the upper jaw where the great teeth of the lower bedded. But the lower jaw, he realized, was beneath him—was, in fact, lifting the boat high from the water.

He turned and leaped headlong toward the bow as

the jaws came together in a great crashing of cedar and ash, splintering the boat and everything in it to matchwood.

He was in a tangle of line and oars and lances, and the bow section was tipping straight down, falling into the sea. He saw little bobbing heads beneath him and arms flailing the churned water—and then the crash!

The chaos was nightmarish underwater. Kicking men, splinters, broken oars, boat spades, sprung kegs and the manila line coiling and whipping everywhere in the whirling eddies.

The water was dark blue smeared with crimson. Directly before Jess was the great blurred shape of the whale's head. Stupidly, in a futile gesture of puny defiance, he reached for his sheath knife. His sweeping left hand caught something that was rising with a lunge and he went up with it.

He broke the surface and found he was grasping a gunwhale. Spewing water, wheezing, his hands clawing at wood for support, he spilled himself over the gunwhale and into a half-flooded boat.

I didn't jump! Blast you, I didn't! He thought he was shouting but he wasn't, couldn't.

Something was wrong. The harpoon line was smoking around the loggerhead and humming out through the bow chock. It couldn't be Ralls's boat; that boat was splinters. Then Starr must have been dumped also. Now everybody was in the water except Jess.

No, not everyone—he saw a man's body jammed under the stroke oar's thwart, pinned underwater. Jess stumble-splashed aft, collided with the whizzing line and it was like being burned by a white-hot branding iron. If left a livid streak on his upper arm. He ducked under the humming warp and caught the man by the hair and raised his head.

George Starr!

The boat jolted. Jess went headlong into the stern-sheets. He turned hurriedly, grabbing for the mate's hair again. A voice that might have belonged to Ralls was shouting from somewhere.

"Jump! Jump, Hanna!"

He didn't. He wrestled with the mate's bulky body, trying to haul it up into his lap, and saw bright red streaks running from Starr's hair. Must have clipped

his head on a gunwale or thwart when the whale dumped his boat over. But he was still breathing.

Jess looked forward and saw the reason for the activated harpoon line. Starr's boat was still attached to the whale—a runaway whale. They were going on the Nantucket sleigh ride.

His knife was gone, the boat's hatchet was missing, but he found a lance submerged on the floorboards. He propped the unconscious mate in the sternsheets and turned to the flying warp to cut it with the razor-bladed lance. Then, indecisively, he stalled.

After a while he put the lance down and picked up a bailer instead and did what he could to get some of the water weight out of the boat.

The harpoon line vibrating like a plucked harpstring, the whaleboat went skimming across the sea with sickening slams from crest to crest and with spray cascading back from the bows. Mile fell into vast mile in the crazy whirling wake of the helpless boat. Jess stopped bailing and sat in a soggy slump.

The singing in the line toned down to a hum and the wisps of blue smoke about the loggerhead vanished. Jess watched the line. It went slack. The whale had stopped. He looked at the mate.

"Ask me for help, Starr," he said. "Go on. Ask me to do your job now that you can't."

He laughed crazily and began hauling the boat along the line.

Hand over hand he hauled in on the line and the boat came ponderously up to the shining black mountain, creeping diagonally astern of the whale, just

safely clear of the slowly threshing flukes. He brought
the bow up to where the harpoon was pronged in the
bull's hump.

He waded forward through a tangle of line, carrying the lance, and braced his left leg against the bow
cleat and raised the lance high over his head. The
gleaming hump swelled up and over and away from
him.

He drove the slender iron shaft six feet into the
whale, putting more than just his weight and strength
into the blow—putting his soul into the lance.

The sun was low and golden weary when Ralls
came up in the third mate's boat. The crew let out a
cheer when they saw the dead sperm whale wallowing
in a distant trough, but hushed when they looked in
Jess's blank face. He wasn't mad—as some first
thought—but in a sort of calm shock.

They grappled the gunwale of the half-submerged
boat and lifted the unconscious Starr aboard. Jess was
sitting slack-armed in the water, staring at the whale.
He made no move to leave the boat until Ralls leaned
over and put a hand on his shoulder.

"It's all right now, lad," he said quietly. "You don't
have to jump, you know. Just step over the gunnel."

Jess still said nothing. He sat in the stern with
Ralls and, as Gant's boat gave way, he looked across
the water.

The dead whale was down on its starboard side, its
larboard fin standing stiff and stark in the air, slab-
like against a milk sky. It was like a monument.

7. Who Needs A Crew When There's No Ship?

STARR OFFERED Jess no thanks for saving his life or for killing the whale. Jess's outstanding action only served to increase the mate's enmity. His ego had suffered a tremendous blow. It was too late, Starr discovered, to try to reinstate Jess as the lowly trypot boy. The seamen, even the harpooners, were singing Jess's. praise, and Ralls vowed he would feed his legs to a spermaceti before he would surrender Jess as his stroke oar. All of which did very little to brighten Starr's black mood.

From the observations and study of the charts Ralls told Jess they were closing the Sumatra coast at a point south of the Mentawai Islands—dangerous ground, because it was patrolled by fierce Javanese

pirates. Starr patronized this most southerly area because it was not so thoroughly combed by the other
American whalers.

They ran at night now, with all lights screened,
and in daylight there were double lookouts posted at
the mastheads, with a standing reward of a pint of rum
to the man who first sighted a whale or a sail.

Starr was more restless, drinking more heavily at
night in his lonely cabin. He remained on deck during
the daylight hours, morose, abstracted, constantly
sweeping the horizon with his glass, calling to the mastheads at frequent intervals.

The crew was tense and sullenly vigilant. The twelve-
pounders were kept ready and unbreeched and powder chests and shot were ranged in the racks under the
boatracks. Jess was conscious of an overpowering
sense of menace, a feeling which Barnaby shared. The
Irishman would wrinkle his nose, sniff the wind and
say:

"Say I'm fey if ye will, Jesse me bhoy, but I smell
trouble. Aye, there's death in the air."

Then he would stroll away, humming a rigadig tune
like a frightened boy whistling in the dark . . .

> "Dance to your daddy,
>   My little laddy,
> Dance to your daddy,
>   My laddy-o!"

Then there was a day of light airs, sultry and sluggish, the sun bubbling the pitch in the deck seams. The
Bunyan was standing southeastward, wing and wing

to catch all the pressure of the light breeze. Suddenly the main masthead hailed the deck.

"*Land oooh!* Three p'ints to larboard!"

Starr went up and studied the landfall from the main crosstrees. When he returned to deck he spoke gruffly to Ralls.

"Looks quiet enough. We'll put in and fill our casks."

Ralls looked startled. "It isn't safe. You can't tell what might be lurking behind those headlands."

"We need water, don't we, mister?" the mate growled.

"Aye—but we should have gotten it at Ceylon. And we could have replenished our crew as well."

"We're getting by with the crew we have," Starr said. "We already have over a thousand barrels of sperm, don't we?"

They stood in for the nameless spot of bush-covered land, which showed a rill of water trickling across a reef. By midafternoon they closed the shore, the central mountain ranges a misty blue barrier in the distance, and came to off the mouth of a lagoon framed in a dense growth of jungle topped by feather-crested palms.

There were no signs of life—but they had barely let go the anchor when a lugger shot around a green point and stood out to them.

The breeze died out—in a hurry, as if it had been waiting for just this to happen. The lugger, manned by a full crew of oarsmen, came like a voracious centipede. The whaler was stuck. Without a wind she couldn't cut and run.

"What are you gutless lubbers trembling in your boots about?" Starr ragged the crew. "We have the twelve-pounders, don't we?"

The main masthead sang out again. "Sail ho! Another one coming out on the starboard quarter!"

And the words had scarcely passed his lips when the fore masthead hailed.

"Deck there! A big 'un coming up on the starboard beam."

Heyday, Jess thought, *three warboats at once!* Standing by the main starboard shrouds he began to discern details. Half garbed in a brilliant miscellany of garments, the slant-eyed pirates shook their weapons—curiously shaped knives and swords, long barbed spears and clumsy antiquated muskets—at the ship. There could be no doubt about it. They meant business—like a batch of sharks ganging up on a dead whale.

Starr handed the key to the arms rack to Ralls, and the second mate ordered Jess and Tavi to go below with him. They didn't see anything of Captain Coffin, who was probably innocently sleeping in his cabin. The door to the mate's cabin hung open and Ralls paused, looking in.

He passed the key to Tavi. "Fetch fella musket," he instructed the Kanaka.

Jess watched the second mate step into Starr's cabin to stare with a certain interest at a chart that the mate had left on his deal table, held flat by parallel rulers and dividers. It was a somewhat accurately detailed chart of the Antarctic Ocean, about which very little was then known.

"What's that for, sir?" Jess was looking over Ralls's shoulder. "I thought you said our course was plotted to pass through the Tasman Sea to the South Pacific?"

"Aye," Ralls murmured. "That's what Captain Coffin told me. Strange."

Very strange. Few ships ever ventured into the Antarctic Circle. Captain Cook was the first man to enter the pack ice back in the 1770's, but he did not see land. The British, in 1820, were the first to actually find land there, and Captain John Davis, an American sealer, was the first man to set foot on the icy continent. That had only been last year: February 1821.

Jess leaned over the table and gazed at the vast uncharted mysterious sea. Even looking at the chart, with its great blank spaces and its lack of soundings, was enough to give a seaman the shivers. The sealers said the icebergs and floe ice in that corner of the world could rip open more hulls and grind the life out of more sailors than any other treacherous spot at sea. It was, they said, especially dangerous in the spring and early summer months because that was when the bergs and floes cracked away from the pack ice and started to drift north.

What did it mean? Starr had no reason to ponder over the sketchy details of the Antarctic's cruel snares on a chart that at best could only be partially accurate. It was a simple matter to give the Antarctic Ocean a wide berth to larboard. Nobody needed a chart to clear an ocean!

The starboard twelve-pounder thumped on deck and the roar of its discharge reverberated through the entire hull of the whaler.

"C'mon!" Ralls said. "They're starting to fight."

The three men struggled on deck with mighty armloads of muskets, boarding pistols and cutlasses, which they quickly served out to all hands. Starr was upbraiding the guncrew something fierce.

"Do you call that shooting? You blubber heads must think we're fighting the island instead of the luggers! You fired three fathoms high! Blast your eyes for moonstones! Depress that gun!"

They were loading now. A man named Return Meigs was sponger, and Abiel Cook stowed home a powder cartridge, then a roundshot on top of it. Barnaby, who had served aboard a king's ship (and had deserted from same), was acting as gunner.

Jess, a musket in his hand, a cutlass and pistol in his belt, glanced overboard.

The pirates were making their boat attack on a wide front—fanning out and coming in sharply right, left and center. They all looked wild, most of them half naked in vivid sarongs, others wearing a panache of varicolored feathers. Now and then one of them would stand up, scream something unintelligible and flourish a knife or sword at the whaler.

Barnaby squinted along the gun, to hold the muzzle right at the center lugger's waterline. He motioned to Pickering, the match man.

"Up wi' the giddy screw a trifle now."

A cautious turn or two and the muzzle was depressed. The match was glowing, lighted, ready.

"What are you waiting for, Barnaby!" Starr bawled. "An invitation? Flukes and flames, man—*fire!*"

Pickering laid the match. The twelve-pounder burst forth flame and smoke and howling roundshot. The gun sprang back like a thing alive and its breeching cable snapped taut, checked the recoil. A cloud of acrid, rotten-smelling heat beat back in Jess's face and for a moment he couldn't see.

A geyser had sprung up and was already plashing back into the water. The remnants of the center lugger were falling with it—scattering arms and legs and weapons in a maelstrom of splintered confusion. The *Bunyan*'s crew cut loose with a mighty cheer.

"Belay!" Starr roared at them. "Have 'ee forgotten the other two? Mr. Gant—take half the crew in the boom and open on that lugger! Mr. Ralls—the other half to the stern! Show some spunk, blast you! Stations! Stations for your lives!"

Jess found himself in a crush of men rushing pell-mell to the whaler's stern. The pirates had used their heads. Once they had lost their center lugger, the other two had swung far out and in, coming at the *Bunyan* stem and stern where Barnaby's gun couldn't reach them. Now they were driving in fast, their many-bladed passage churning the water to froth.

Jess climbed up on the little stern boatdeck over the wheel and knelt down and opened fire with his musket.

The Javanese, a gaunt, tawdry rabble screaming and rowing and brandishing their vivid assortment of weapons, pulled into the musketry and bullets peppered the water all around them. They kept on coming—some of them spilling overboard, others kicking around on the floorboards; they passed through the lead hailstorm and under the counter of the whaler.

And, abruptly, they were scrabbling over the taffrail like screeching wildcats, thrusting with the *irkrises* and jabbing with their boarding spears. The whalemen fired their pistols into the pack and waded in to meet blade with blade. Starr was like a madman, bellowing and slashing, hook and cutlass.

Two Javanese came clawing over the edge of the boatdeck and Jess gave the first one a direct potshot, bowling him over like a colorful rag doll. He pitched his smoking pistol in the second one's face and slashed at him with his cutlass—and suddenly there were two more dancing, yelling pirates on the deck with him.

It was like a nightmare where no matter how many enemies you kill there is always another to take his place, and another and another. Jess leaped and wheeled and cut and lunged; and gradually he realized he was being backed up to the edge of the deck. The lagoon yawned under him.

From the waist came the shout of the enraged first mate, and all at once the Javanese found themselves caught between two fires. Gant's gang had discouraged the lugger that had hoped to swarm over the bow and it had pulled off sullenly. Now Gant's men were

streaming across the deck to drive full at the pirates
who were fighting Ralls's party.

Only one pirate was left facing Jess, a slim clean-
faced youth, his glittering eyes set obliquely in his olive
face. He raised his long *kris* to break off the combat,
stepped back and glanced around at the deck below,
taking in the hopeless situation instantly. He flashed
a quick grin at Jess, tossed his *kris* aside and made a
short running dive over the edge of the boatdeck. Jess
watched him hit the water as clean as a knife.

The pirates were piling over the stern in a scrambling rush as if pursued by a pack of hunger-wild lions.
But they were totally out of luck. Several triangular
slate-gray fins were now cutting the lagoon's surface
in quick, adroit maneuvers which brought them closer
and closer to the swimming Javanese.

By threes and fives the sharks congregated and
went to work. Within minutes the screaming, thrashing, frantic water became a crimson bath as the voracious fish darted here and there, dreadfully swift, turning over on their backs with a flash of their white bellies, and snapping and then rolling upright and slipping gracefully away, dragging the struggling, yowl-
ing pirates under.

"Mr. Gant! Mr. Ralls!" Starr called. "Clear the ship
of the rats. The dead go overside!"

Some of the fallen Javanese, Jess noticed, were not
dead, merely wounded. It didn't signify with Starr.
"Pitch the vermin overboard!" he ordered.

Jess stared at the turbulent lagoon for a long moment, wondering what had happened to the young

Javanese pirate who had grinned at him before diving overboard. The shore seemed a long way off.

"I hope he makes it," he thought.

The mountains of Sumatra were swallowed up in the sunset glow and the shore breeze, strengthening as the twilight darkened, wafted the *Bunyan* along on its fragrant bosom. The stars crept into the winy sky and shone in tropic splendor, and night settled down like a gentle benediction.

At such a moment it was difficult for Jess to believe that so much evil could exist on land and sea, that he had fought blade to blade with a crew of throat-cutting pirates, and that he had to rub shoulders with an abysmal brute like George Starr. But he knew that the peacefulness around him and the ship was only illusory . . . .

He was standing the midwatch at the wheel. Gant, the deck officer, had wandered somewhere forward. The skylight had been raised to catch a whiff of wind in the cuddy below, and Jess could hear the mate and Ralls going at it hammer and tongs over the fiddle table.

"That you're up to some game or other is as plain as the nose on your face, Starr," Ralls said.

"You interest me, mister. Rave on."

"Aye—I'll rave, and you'll answer. For a long time there's been talk about how Captain Morse fell overboard on the last voyage—talk about whether it was really an accident."

"Fo'c'sle talk," Starr said belittlingly.

"Maybe. But what about the fire that almost destroyed the ship on her last leg of that voyage? If I hadn't rousted the crew when I did, this hooker would have been lost."

"Why worry about it, mister? She *wasn't* lost, was she?"

"No—but I think to no thanks to you. All right, let's take this voyage we're on now. Why did we go to sea with a skipper so old and infirm that he can't remember fore from aft? And why were you and the steward discussing him with the owner in a New Bedford barn before we sailed?"

"Ha! So the Jumping Jack told you about that, did he? All right, mister. I'll answer your question if that'll settle your hash for you. Captain Coffin is a friend of Mr. Munro's. The old man wanted to make one final voyage, and the owner didn't have the heart to refuse him. So Munro told me and the steward to keep an eye on the old duffer. That's all—just a kindly eye."

"It won't wash, Starr. I know Munro. He doesn't worry about old skippers who have drifted into the boneyard. He worries about every penny and shilling he has in the bank. Nothing more. But we'll pass that for the moment and come to something more pertinent. Why do you insist on sailing so shorthanded, and why have you secretly been studying a chart of the Antarctic Ocean?"

Just then Mr. Gant strolled back to the wheel for a look in the binnacle, and Jess lost Starr's reply.

Gant studied the compass course and glanced at the sails to make sure they were drawing full.

"Keep your eye on the mainpeak, Jumping Jack. You're luffing your course," he growled.

"Eye on the mainpeak it is, sir," Jess said mechanically.

The third mate stalked away, and Jess leaned forward to catch more of the conversation in the cuddy through the skylight.

"But that's barratry!" Ralls's voice.

"Call it what you will, mister, it's worth a fortune. And you better splice in if you know what's good for you. Gant has, and Jack Hay *was* in—until somebody put out his lamp for him. It was his job to take care of the old man."

"Man alive, it won't work! What about the crew?"

"The crew? Ha! You need to calk your brain, mister. Who needs a crew when there's no ship?"

"Good Lord, Starr! You're talking of mass—"

"Avast!" Starr hissed. "The giddy skylight's open. Who's on the wheel?"

"I don't know. It's Gant's watch."

Boots clomped up the steps and the companionway door shot open and Starr glowered out at Jess.

"So it's you, is it, Jumping Jack? Laying an ear to my business again, eh?"

Jess adopted a stupidly innocent pose.

"Pardon, sir? Listening to you? No, sir. I could hear voices below, but not what you were saying. I've had my eye on the mainpeak, like Mr. Gant ordered."

Starr lumbered over to stand beside Jess, the light from the binnacle casting a satanic expression over his forceful face.

"Aye," he growled, "and a good thing it is, too. You've had an ear in my affairs before and got off lucky I didn't gut you."

Jess said nothing. He kept his eye on the compass card.

"You just keep your port shut, Hanna, and maybe I won't use you for shark bait. Maybe!"

The mate spun on his heel and disappeared below. A moment later the skylight clattered shut. Jess let out his breath. He counted himself lucky—because he was certain that Starr knew he *had* heard the conversation in the cuddy.

I'll never live to see the end of this voyage, he thought. *Not if Starr has his way.* And, from what he had overheard, none of the crew would live to reach home port again.

Barratry was an old and dirty dodge at sea. It meant to deliberately destroy a ship or its cargo in order to defraud the underwriters and collect on the insurance. That's why Munro had said the job had to be done with a full cargo or the game wouldn't be worth the candle. The *Bunyan* alone was possibly worth $25,000, and a full cargo of sperm oil would fetch at least $40,000.

A neat little nest egg when split between the owner and the mate and perhaps a third party!

How much the whaler was insured for, and why the underwriters would venture to insure such a bad-luck ship, were questions beyond Jess's knowledge. There was no point in wondering over the actions of underwriters. They would risk a dollar anytime to earn a shilling, and by some uncanny manipulation they invariably saved their dollar too.

One thing he knew, Underwriters were a skeptical

lot. They didn't open their purses and pour out gold without question when some tired old whaler went down. The wrecking of the *Bunyan* would have to be done artistically if profit were to accrue to her owner and to Starr. And Jess thought he could see some advance signs of that artistry already . . . .

Mr. Munro had engaged Captain Coffin to command his ship; a man so old and infirm that he wasn't capable of commanding a washtub, let alone a 300-ton whaler! But—Captain Coffin undoubtedly had a clean record for his forty years at sea, and the underwriters would not question his word. And Captain Coffin was the man who kept the log, who made all the entries showing just how much sperm oil had been taken aboard his ship. The underwriters would accept the old man's log as gospel.

So—all Starr had to do was dispose of Captain Coffin and the crew and ship, but keep the log to turn over to Mr. Munro.

"And he can take care of all three very nicely in the Antarctic Ocean," Jess thought. "It's a simple thing to lose a ship for good in the pack ice."

He thought about the feeble old man who was being led like a lamb to the slaughter. Like all young men, especially young seamen, Jess had a certain intolerance for doddering old skippers who clung too long to the weather side of the quarterdeck. Command was no office for the sickly and withered. And, too, Jess had his own life to worry about.

Yet the sporting blood in him sided with Captain Coffin. The old man's body and mind had worn out,

but he was still striving to do the impossible, to maintain command—in his helpless way—over a torpid
body and mind and a bad-luck ship, never dreaming
that Starr was using him, duping him, and would soon
destroy him.

"More than a dying body and a dying ship are lined
up against him," Jess reflected as the *Bunyan* plowed
on into the dark crisp sea.

The next morning Mr. Ralls was missing.

8. We'll Kill till We've A Full Hold of Sperm!

"OVERBOARD," Starr remarked offhandedly to the group of harpooners and seamen who had searched the ship alow and aloft for the missing second mate.

"I've seen it happen before to his sort," he went on to say. "It's a way the quiet moody ones have."

"Are you saying it was suicide, Mr. Starr?" Jess asked.

The mate's chipped ice eyes centered on Jess's face.

"Aye, my son. Suicide's the word for it."

"I don't believe it. Not Ralls!"

"*N-o?*" Starr drawled the word. "And what is it you believe, bucko?" His voice was like his eyes, cold and dangerous.

"You and he had an argument in the cuddy last night, and you—"

Gant snatched a pocket pistol from his jacket.

"That's enough of that, Jumping Jack!" he snarled. "Seamen have been shot for saying less!"

A blazing orgasm of fury boiled over in Jess. He hadn't felt anything quite like it since his speechless anger days in the orphanage when he was very little. Ralls had been his one true friend aboard the ill-starred whaler, had stuck by him through thick and thin. And now Starr had put him overboard—had killed him.

It was too much to take. And having Gant threaten him with that blasted pistol was the iron that broke the whale's back.

"How long are you going to let them beat you and starve you and kill you off one by one?" he yelled at the crew. "If you had the backbone of a flea you'd take 'em in one rush!"

The crew started to mutter, to grumble—someone reached for a belaying pin, a hand drew a sheath knife. The three harpooners ranged around Starr and Gant, pulling their knives. Starr flashed his pistol at Jess.

"Inciting a mutiny, eh Hanna?" he snarled. "There's just one answer to that—"

"*SHE BLOOOWS!*" the masthead wailed. "Blows to starboard and sparm at that! A school a sparm! *There! There!*"

Animosity instantly vanished. Threat of mutiny and death went by the boards. Ralls's disappearance was forgotten. Sperm whales had spouted and it was the whaleman's job to lower and after!

"To the boats, blast ye!" Starr roared, and he threw his pistol aside. "Lower away the starboard! Lower! Lower!"

The main topsail was thrown aback as all hands rushed to the lowering boats. Jess reached the starboard bow boat, then remembered they no longer had a mate to command and steer. Starr came racing across the deck spewing orders like a wildman.

" 'Lisha! Take the wheel! Bring down the masthead! Where's that cooper? I want him in the boats! The cook goes too! Every son of Satan goes!"

He paused and glared at the second mate's bewildered boat crew.

"Barnaby, take command of the bow boat! If you foul your job, I'll break your Irish head! Lower away!"

"A dead whale or a stove boat!" The whalemen yelled.

In less than three minutes every boat was in the water and heading for the whales, and every pound of strength that was in the muscles of the seamen was being thrown into the oars until the boats fairly flew through the water.

"Heave and haul — long and hard!" Barnaby chanted in the sternsheets. "Crack yer backs, bust yer innards, me fine laddy'os! We've run in the cabin, greasy sparm in the hold—who wouldn't drink to fortune and pledge the whaler bold! Heave and haul! Start my soul bolts, but 'tis grannies ye are! Don't 'ee know what the giddy oars is for? Heave is what I'm telling yez!"

All at once Jess could hear the *shooo-shooo* of a

sperm whale's scalding vapor spouting from its blow-hole and, out of the corner of his eye, caught a quick glimpse of fluctuating flukes.

"Return Meigs!" Barnaby hissed at the tub oar, "I'll rap yer head loose at the neck if ye look again! Sure and you know better than to peek when pulling on to a whale!"

Without warning, their boat was suddenly between two big whales; over a hundred barrels each. "Between cedar wood and black skin," in whaling parlance. By reaching over, Jess could have placed his hand on one of the huge bulls.

"Stand up, Nehemiah!" Barnaby ordered.

But something was drastically wrong—at least for Nehemiah, who was only a harpooner by default. He was used to making a bow-dart with his iron, and now the boat was too close to the whale to allow clearance to turn bow-in.

"Hoo-ee! Strike, Nehemiah me bhoy!" Barnaby cried.

Nehemiah became gallied—couldn't think straight. He was too close for darting and instead of driving or setting his iron into the leviathan solid, he drove it at him obliquely, cutting the bull down the side. Catching up his second iron he wildly pitch-poled it clear over the whale's hump.

"Loosh! Did 'ee see that now!" Barnaby wailed.

The harpooned whale didn't sound as it was supposed to do. It swerved to the right and expelled a great rolling diapason of air and rage. It's a peculiar fact that as soon as one whale in a pod is ironed all

the rest know it; instantly there was a waterquake all
around the boat—a seething mass of white water and
heads and flukes and fins in every direction.

"Stern all!" Barnaby cried. "Saints and sinners de-
liver uz from this inferno!"

Jess's oarblade skittered at the foam-lashed water
and swung wildly in the air as the stern lurched up on a
whale-tossed wave—now out of sight of the bull as
they made the sweeping passage to the crest, again
gawking down at the shimmering hump of the brute
from the summit of the watery hill, and then down
they came and the larboard whale was waiting for
them.

The bull towered over the bows like a leaning house,
its upper jaw as broad and flat as the counter on a
whaler, and Jess knew that nineteen-foot-long sickle-
shaped lower jaw was under them; and, as from far
away, he heard Tavi yell, "Fella whale walkabout too
much!"

Then the bull's mouth crunched right through the
splintering bows and everyone was screaming and Jess
figured that Nehemiah and Tavi had both gone the
way of Jonah, and the next thing he knew he and
Barnaby were in a canted, half-flooded boat with the
tub-line wrapped around them.

The bow had been sheered completely off and Tavi
was in the water and swimming back to the swamped
boat—and when Jess looked up he nearly screamed.

The whale's monstrous rearing head blacked out
the sky over them, and Nehemiah was away up there
dangling out of the whale's slowly closing mouth!

Sprawled across that gangplanklike lower jaw, pinioned on the six-inch teeth, his arms waving helplessly at his shipmates who were tumbling about in the remnants of their boat below him, Nehemiah started to scream.

He tried to twist about and work himself loose, his arms flailing wildly, only to find himself hopelessly snared in the crotch of the whale's jaw along with jagged plank splinters and snapped oars and even a bent lance. Then the mighty jaws closed and for a vivid instant Nehemiah's face looked like a squeezed grape.

The whale's enormous head came down and crashed like thunder into the sea.

"There go flukes!"

There went Nehemiah too—and in a moment there would go Jess and Barnaby! Jess was so shocked by horror that it took him a few seconds to remember that he and Barnaby were enmeshed in the deadly network of harpoon line.

He saw the slack coils of the floating manila line start to duck into the sea and suddenly realized that he was snarled in the whipping coils like a fly in a spider's web. It was around his arms and legs and neck, and Barnaby, caught in the maze with him, was calling on his patron saint to intercede for him and the quicker the better! In another minute that line would snatch them down into the mute blue depths and decapitate them or strangle them or simply let them drown.

They struggled frenziedly to clear themselves, but

they were completely entangled in the clinging coils and there was no one else left in the boat to help them —and the line was disappearing faster and faster.

Tavi breaststroked into the half-submerged boat where the bow had once been. Reaching for an awash thwart he hauled himself clear of the tangled clot of running line and glanced aft at Jess and Barnaby, instantly perceiving their predicament.

Unable to rise to a standing position he bellyflopped back into the water and grabbed a loose turn in the floating line. Treading water, he bit into the manila line with his teeth and fumbled underwater for his sheath knife. Suddenly his head snapped to the left and was yanked out of sight.

Horrified, Jess saw the Kanaka vanish below the surface. Then he felt the deadly coils wrapped around his body start to life. Barnaby screamed. Tavi's hand and knife leaped from the water and his head bobbed to the surface. The line was free!

Jess sagged in the waterlogged sternsheets of the whaleboat. He felt like a gutted halibut in a pan of water. Pie-face swam over to join them by the awash gunwale, and then the fifth man, Return Meigs, dogpaddled up to the stern. The last man, Nehemiah, would never return to the boat.

Mr. Gant's boat picked them up. Gant had killed a whale and the great dead carcass was rolling in a trough of the sea, fin out, about an eighth of a mile astern.

"Lively!" he bawled at the shipwrecked men. "Lay

away on them oars! We'll have to tow my kill to the
ship."

"Fins out to larb'rd!" Levi Munson, Gant's harpooner, called.

The seamen looked around and saw two more fins
standing out of the sea in the east. Starr had evidently
enjoyed greasy luck. Two kills! The mate's boat was
bearing down on them rapidly.

"Belay that course, mister!" Starr bawled at Gant.
"Never mind your kill now. There's still whales to be
had out here!"

Gant looked at him apprehensively. "You want
more? We've already lost a hand and a boat!"

"Aye, more and still more!" Starr's arctic eyes were
bright with passion. "We'll kill till we've a full hold of
sperm!"

"But that whale that got the bow boat is a killer!"

"And so am I, mister!" Starr roared. "Now belay all
talk and ship two of the survivors to my boat. Look
alive, blast you!"

They were off again, two boats this time, scrabbling
like fury after the pod of whales in a stern chase. Then
everything that could go wrong on a whale hunt *did*
go wrong, and all at once. A majestic fan of iridescent
spray spouted from the sea ahead of Starr's boat and
the whale Nehemiah had ironed rose tremendously to
the surface and seemed to scan the sea for his puny
enemies.

Spotting Starr's boat, he gave a mighty whack with
his tail and started straight for the mate. His great black
head driving the waves before it, like the broad bow

of a barge, loomed high and menacing. But Starr was a madman. He elected to rush headlong into the oncoming jaws of death.

"Heave all! Spring and start her!"

His boat crew, not being allowed to look, didn't know what they were headed for. They laid back on the oars and the boat lifted along through the water, with Starr holding them head on for the charging whale.

Coolly, as if he were coming alongside the *Bunyan,* the mate jammed the steering oar over and swung the boat at right angles to her course, then brought her back again with another broad sheer as the whale foamed past him.

This maneuver brought the leviathan directly between the two boats. Jess glanced to larboard and saw the looming head and hump of the great whale rushing by close aboard with its mouth open and showing its livid throat and fearsome teeth along its lower jaw. Then Starr's boat shot over to starboard and passed out of sight on the far side of the whale, but they heard his raucous voice.

"Give it to him, Jekiel! Plant your iron!"

"Stand up, Levi!" Gant cried at his harpooner, hoping to share in Starr's kill. He bent to the steering oar and the bow swung over to face the black shining mass of the whale.

Levi barely had a chance to make his dart. Starr's harpooner had already struck and now the inevitable quake exploded. There was an upheaval of the sea dead ahead as the vast tail of the bull rose terrifically into the air, streaming rivulets of water—up up, still higher, until the whole immense spread of the flukes, fifteen feet from tip to tip, hung on high, apparently motionless—and then let go.

"Starn all! Starn for—"

A ton of living flesh swooped down like a flying black wedge. It whistled over Jess's ducked head and caught Gant's stroke oar, Tom Pickering, on the back of the head with a crushing *thh-omp!* and whisked him out of the boat before Jess's terrified eyes.

On either side of that mountainous mass the waters rose in shining towers of snowy foam which fell splashing back into the sea like waterfalls, whirling and eddying around the boat as it tossed and fell like a chip in a millrace.

Blinded by the flying spray, four men backstroking for their lives, Jess and Barnaby bailing furiously to free the boat of the water she had shipped, it was a moment before they could collect their wits and look around to see what was happening.

Instead of sounding as he had before, the ironed whale was lying astern of the two boats. His enormous tail lifted from the water and, with wide-spread flukes, started fluttering horizontally over the surface, carefully feeling for the boats. If those sensitive flukes touched anything except water the bull would instantly hammer it to pulp with his mighty tail.

But that maniac Starr was looking for a kill!

"After him! All hands lively!"

"Take stroke oar," Gant ordered Pie-face. "Come aft, Levi!"

Stumbling and cursing through the confusion of the overcrowded boat, the third mate and his harpooner changed positions and Gant picked up a lance. Starr was already well on his way, his boat crawling quickly astern of those great waving flukes which were delicately feeling over the waves. The mate put his steering oar to larboard and started cautiously around the starboard side of the great bull.

It was the wrong moment. Unable to find a thing with his flukes the whale lowered his tail and started to come about broadside, to use his eyes instead. He barely touched Starr's boat with the first flirt of his tail.

Instantly the huge tail swept away from the mate's boat. Rising straight up, the mighty mass of gristle leaped into the sunshine like a vast tossed shadow. It curved back from the boat like a hammer cocked over a blacksmith's shoulder.

"Stern all!"

Too late. Jekiel and the bow oarsman sprang wildly overboard as the tremendous tail came at them with a roar, released like a spring from its tons of tension. It caught the mate's boat full on the broadside, sending all hands flying out of the crashing splinters as if fired from catapults.

In a quick, orderly manner the enraged bull swung off to starboard and started flailing the sea with his smashing flukes, to finish off the men who were now scattered in the water amidst the shattered planks and snapped oars and lance poles and the endless coils of tangled tub-line.

As much as Jess hated Gant he had to give the man credit for courage now. The third mate was a good whaleman; he knew his job. He was going to try to distract the bull's attention and give Starr's boat crew a chance to escape that crushing tail.

"Pull, blast your bolts! Stroke and stroke and stroke again! Heave, blust your sogering souls! Carry away something!"

The sending whaleboat bounded in at the furious bull who was churning the sea into yeasty foam over an enormous area. They came wallowing in on the whale's larboard—right into the heart of the turmoil as if begging for disaster. Close upon him now, Gant —the lance ready in his hands—yelled aft at Munson.

"Lay off! Off with her, Levi!"

The boat sheered out a bit till they were abreast of the whale's thrashing flukes. "Beach me!" Gant screamed, and the boat lifted with a surge and struck the great blubbery skin. They all heard the *tunk* of the lance as Gant drove it home.

Jess looked forward. Gant was standing in the bow, fanatically churning the oval point of the lance around and around inside the monster, digging for the vital spot.

There was a whirl in the bloody water as the whale rolled away from the boat with a bellow of pain. Gant couldn't disengage the lance in time and he was snatched out of the boat with a cry. Once again the far-spread flukes swung into the air.

Levi Munson forgot to yell *Stern All!* but it didn't matter because Jess and the rest were already trying desperately to bury their blades in the foaming water to work clear. Jess had barely got a bite with his blade on something that felt enough like solid water to start to back, when the monster's gleaming bulk reared smack alongside and flung the starboard oars apart with a sound like pistol shots.

The flukes recurved with a sidelong sweep, like a gigantic scythe, and the chopping blow shored off the bow of Gant's boat as if it had been an eggshell.

Just at that wrong moment Munson stooped and picked up the tub-line from its turn round the logger-head and threw it forward. In his excitement he gave a twist with his hand and the whizzing line whipped out a kink and looped around Pie-face's neck—as the whale sounded with a splattering rush.

Struggling, his face hideously contorted, neck muscles standing strongly out, clutching at the fatal noose, Pie-face went flying helplessly out through the incoming water, and in one second he was on his way to the bottom of the sea.

"Cut line! Cut line!" Barnaby cried.

Jess snatched up a boat hatchet, shoved Munson aside and swung the blade savagely at the humming manila line where it smoked around the loggerhead. The line parted with a crack.

Quickly the seamen stretched their oars athwart and lashed them to the gunwales to keep the foundering boat afloat. Barnaby spotted a weedylike batch of hair undulating alongside and caught it up. It was Gant, unconscious and half drowned.

"Leave the bucko be," somebody growled from amidship. "Leave him drown."

"Haul him aboard!" Levi Munson cried. "Haul, I say!" The harpooner seemed batchy with fear and emotion.

Jess leaned over and gave Barnaby a hand with the third mate.

Slowly, painfully, Starr and the survivors of his boat crew swam through the swirling froth of wreckage to Gant's waterlogged boat. Two men were missing: the cook and the cooper. The pounding flukes had found them in the red water.

"They didn't even know how to swim," Jekiel Galpin muttered to Jess. "Starr had no right to order 'em into the boats."

9. The Dead Go Overside

Two BOATS destroyed, one disabled, and five men dead. Quite a victory—for the leviathans.

The crew was discouraged and disgusted, weary and surly. They blamed Starr for the grim results of the day. Their attitude only served to enrage the mate's elated sense of ego. He could do no wrong, ever. He had to be right, always. Nothing could possibly be his fault.

He hazed them unmercifully, driving them through the cutting-in process, to the blubber room, to the mincing trough, to the trypots. He gave them no rest, no respite from his cursing and his rope-end; if any man complained or started to lag at his labor, Starr went after him with his fist and boots. The men were disheartened and terrified.

"If you had the guts of a scurvy mouse you'd mutiny," Jess said in disgust.

'Lisha Nook, Jehiel Galpin, Abiel Cook and Return Meigs were too demoralized to respond. They simply shook their heads when Jess tried to instill a spark of courage in them, and hunkered abjectly over their slop pans, gulping their food like worn-out animals.

Tavi lived in a quiet little world comprised of himself alone. He kept his own counsel, never said a word, never even seemed to listen. And Barnaby, though he was a fighting Irishman on land, had spent too many years on the sea to entertain any wild notions about rebelling against authority. Sea law had been calked into his soul with a mallet.

But there was this to be said about Barnaby: he could easily recognize and appreciate the fighting spirit in Jess that refused to knuckle under to a brute like Starr. And though he was seemingly unable to stand up for his own rights, he was quite willing to help Jess stand up for his.

"You seem set on getting into a rough and tumble wi' the mate, Jesse lad. But there's things 'ee should know afore ye do. I've seen ye in action with him once, ye'll mind? And it come over me ye didn't rightly know how to use yer hands. Not many Americans do, and that's a fact. For 'tis all tricks, nothing more."

Barnaby grinned and tapped his own red nose.

"Take me, now. 'Tis meself that knows the way of it. Hit at me dial where I stand. Go on, bucko. Ye can't hurt me."

Jess hesitated, glancing around at the other men in the fo'c'sle. 'Lisha Nook spoke from his bunk.

"Go on, Hanna. Stretch the Irisher on the deck!"

Jess cocked his right arm and threw a fairly good blow at Barnaby's jaw. But the jaw wasn't there. Without shifting position, the Irishman swayed his head aside and simultaneously his open right hand flashed up flush under Jess's chin.

"Do 'ee see what I mean now? Sure a man that knows the ins and outs of boxing can deck a bigger, stronger man every try. And 'tis what ye'll be needing the next time you cross courses with a wicked fighter like Starr."

"Will you teach me, Gypo?" Jess asked.

"Losh! 'Tis no great chore." Barnaby's teeth flashed in a white grin. "Only a matter of time and hard knocks. But fair warning! I'll make 'ee sweat blood, so I will."

"Start swinging," Jess said.

So that night and every night afterward as the old spouter pounded down the West Australian Current, the bare feet of the two men slapped and stamped over the fo'c'sle's deck—Jess and Barnaby panting and grunting and jabbing left-left-left-right, with the others sitting in their bunks and cheering them on.

There were few knockdowns, though often enough one or the other would go stumbling or crashing against the bunk tiers; and Jess didn't actually sweat blood as Barnaby had promised, but many a time he left off with a groggy head and black-and-blue ribs.

Gradually he felt that he was growing harder, faster on his feet and with his hands, and he was beginning to notice that it was more and more difficult for Barnaby to tag him with a punch and to avoid Jess's counterpunches. It would be a different story, of course, when it came to Starr. The mate was a natural fighter and he fought for keeps. He would follow no rules, and fair play were two words he had never heard of.

I've got to beat him, Jess thought. *Not just with my fists—but at the game he's playing as well.*

One day the favoring winds died and the *Bunyan* penetrated the dreaded doldrums. Windless seas were the curse of the whalers who had to go where the whale veins led them. All trade crossing the lonely oily waters of the Equator must encounter doldrums, but merchant or warship heading to or from the Cape of Good Hope could meet them at a minimum of disadvantage, running north or south to pick up the trade winds. The whalers, however, frequently had to quarter the trades to follow the pods, and so there were grim times when the doldrums gripped them for days or weeks under a baking sun.

Nothing could be done about it except to whistle for a wind (which seldom produced any results) to break the calm, and to take advantage of the occasional wisps of wind called cat's paws. For the doldrums might exist in one specific locality and be conspicuously absent only a few miles off, where the variable trades exerted a regional influence.

The luckless *Bunyan* blundered into one of those windless belts in the midwatch of a blistering day. The wind faded and died as if the soul of the sea had turned over in its watery bed and expired. The sails banged and slatted and the whaler rolled on a swell that was emphasized by the lack of wind.

The sun hammered and the air became damp, sultry, oppressive, smothering the ship like a blanket of exhaust from the trypot furnaces. The sky was solid, cloudless.

The seamen dropped out of their bunks and tromped topside to lie on the parched deck half naked. Sometimes they would throw buckets of tepid seawater over each other, which did little good. Starr restricted them to two trips aft a day to the scuttlebut, allowing each man but half a pint of water. Once when Abiel Cook tried to sneak an extra swallow while on watch, Starr had him flogged.

Gant seemed to wilt like a dying flower under the merciless sun. Starr stayed below and brooded over his rum; and old Captain Coffin wobbled about in the main cabin, so desiccated in body and mind that neither heat nor cold seemed to have any effect on him.

After a week of this inferno torture a cat's paw crept up on the whaler's stern and Gant called up the watch and set them to shifting sails to catch it. It was always hard to tell where an errant breeze might push a ship. The whaler lumbered forward and was checked by the swell and fell over on the other tack. It wasn't easy to manage a cat's paw in the doldrums.

Starr appeared on deck and started bellowing orders.

"Man the braces! Trim those headsails closer! Don't you lubbers know how to work out of a calm?"

They were trimmed and the whaler fell off. The

helmsman caught her with the helm as Starr continued to rag the crew.

"Let her off! Four men aloft with hand lines! The rest of you start passing fire buckets up to 'em! Wet down them sails and help 'em draw! Jump, blast your bolts!"

The buckets were hauled to the mastheads and the sails were sprinkled. Just in time; the cat's paw was flicking at the swell astern. Starr stamped up and down the waist, his icy eyes sparking cold fire. Abiel Cook came in his path in a bewildered hurry and the mate hooked him across the deck and into the scuppers for no reason at all. Abiel, half senseless, rolled over and groaned, his bare back trickling blood.

Jess watched this quick incident from the mizzen outrigger and grimaced. Some men, he thought grimly, needed killing. And he reckoned Starr was one of them.

Starr roved the deck like a madman, lashing at the men with a rope-end.

"Pass them buckets! Start 'em, blast you for sogers! Flukes and flames, George Starr'll show you how to look lively!"

He caught Barnaby's shoulder with his hook and swung him around.

"Aye aye, sir," Barnaby babbled. "Quick as a cat, sir!"

Starr swung his fist and rammed a punishing blow into Barnaby's face. The Irish seaman collapsed in a heap.

Something went out of whack in Jess's control. A
wave of red washed across his brain and he grabbed
for the cap backstay to come streaking down to the
deck. But at that moment something pushed at his
back and flowed over his head. He turned to look
around. Seconds later he was hailing the deck.

"Deck there! Wind off the starboard quarter!"

No cat's paw this time; an honest full-bodied breeze
with a good shove behind it. Again all animosity
was immediately forgotten as all hands united their
effort to capture the wind for the good of the ship.

It was a strange thing, Jess reflected later, that as
treacherous as the sea could be, it was at the same time
a great pacifier.

The *Bunyan* labored out of the doldrums with the
fair wind she had picked up south of the Line. She
scudded along under full sail day after day, the blue-
green swells foaming under her cut-water and the
great Australian continent following along off her larboard beam like a distant line of low blue-hazy clouds.

They could only lower two boats now, yet they managed to kill four sperm whales in a fortnight without
the loss of a man or a boat. They seemed to be in greasy
luck. But perhaps it was too greasy . . . .

A few more big oil-yielding kills and the *Bunyan*
would have a full cargo in her hold; the kind of cargo
that would make the game worth the candle to Mr.
Munro and the mate. And every day now brought
them closer to the treacherous Antarctic Ocean—
where Starr would make his play.

It was impossible for Jess to anticipate the full details of Starr's scheme, but he could readily understand
the overall machinations of the plot. The wrecking of
the *Bunyan* required convincing details to make it ring
true in a court of inquiry. And what court or under-
writer would dare suspect trickery or connivance if the
ship's master went down with her?

Starr would need a few witnesses, of course, to help
strengthen his story; Gant was already in the scheme,
and the mate would probably save the two harpooners
Jekiel Burr and Levi Munson. But as for the rest of
the crew . . . .

The thing that puzzled Jess was how would Starr
save his own neck once he scuttled the ship? Wouldn't
he necessarily find himself lost in the barren wilderness of pack ice? The mate must have worked out
some feasible plan to enable him to return to civiliza-
tion, but what could it be?

From the latitude of western Australia Starr set a
course to the southeast, fetching a wide berth around
the continent. The *Bunyan*'s luck held. The weather
was brisk and the wind generally favorable. Porpoises,
harpooned by Jekiel Burr, were served up as sea-pig
to the satisfaction of the ever-hungry crew; Tavi was
now filling in as ship's cook.

It was when they were well south of the West Australian Current that Starr altered the *Bunyan*'s intended course for the Tasman Sea. It wasn't much by
the compass—just enough to set them in the lower
sweep of the Antarctic Current. Then, out of a cloudless sky, the glass started to fall.

By forenoon the wind had become puffy and the whaler was beginning to plunge uncertainly, the sails banging and slatting. The sun continued to shine, but there was an ominous brassy glint to it. Then clouds started scampering across the sky in high-piled disorder, and when the barometer abruptly dropped to thirty-seven, they knew they were in for dirty weather.

"All hands on deck!" Starr roared. "'Man the braces!"

Lifelines were rigged fore and aft and all movable equipment was lashed fast. The wind petered out while the rolling swells continued to rock the whaler like a cork. The sky was drained of color and took on a poisonous leaden hue. The sun was like a great brass song. The air was dead, as if all life had been vacuumed out of it by a great pressure.

"Mr. Gant!" Starr ordered. "I'll have all fore and mainsails furled, stopped and double-lashed! Lash the mizzen boom for a starboard tack!"

The *Bunyan* wallowed about for a bit because of the loss of her great spreads of canvas amidships, but 'Lisha Nook, spinning the wheelspokes handily, accustomed her to ride the steadying influence of the spanker and jibs.

There was a dead calm now, but the *Bunyan* tossed on the swell as though she wanted to roll on her beam ends. Astern, the sky was pitchy black from horizon's end to horizon's end, hovering over the troubled sea like a monstrous dark canopy—heaped to the zenith and toppling forward.

Starr lashed 'Lisha to the wheel and distributed

lengths of line to the rest of the crew, ordering them to secure themselves to lifelines or rigging.

The barometer dropped to a sickening twenty-nine as Jess hurried forward, and when he glanced at the nimbus sky it seemed to him that they were fleeing out of a great tarnished copper bowl. Almost immediately the thrumming harp song of the wind in the cordage started. Then the soul of the sea rolled over with a great sigh and for a moment it was as though the whaler had burst through a giant pane of glass.

There was an awesome shimmering between the sky and the sea—a growth of the conflicting pressure—and Jess heard Barnaby yell at him.

"Saints above. We're in the eye of a typhoon, so we are!"

The spanker was puffed out of existence like a piece of gossamer, and the *Bunyan* wallowed aimlessly off course and humped over as if she meant to search out the hidden bottom.

Jess clung tenaciously to his line by the starboard bow shrouds until a skull-splitting roar such as might have been caused by the collapse of a mountain broke over him; then the headsails were ripped from the ringbolts and came skittering back at him and he went with them—dark sky and white sails all blurring, balling together in his swimming eyes—and he slammed against the larboard monkey rail.

Through the tangle of cordage he saw Barnaby scoot across the deck with his legs cut from under him as if he had been struck by flukes. Jess gained his feet, hearing Starr's voice in the murk.

"Bring her head into it! *Her head, 'Lisha!"*

For a wild moment, in the midst of great whirls and sucks and eddies, Jess felt like laughing. *Into what part of it?* he wondered. *We've got the whole blasted sea and sky down on us!*

He heard somebody shout and, as he turned, he saw a huge darksome mass of glassy water hanging over the larboard bow. But not for long. It toppled with a crash and it felt as though he had been hit by a house.

Airless, blinded, equilibrium shattered, he felt the water grabbing, tugging, hurrying him away—then slam the side of the starboard bulwark. His fingers automatically started to dig for purchase, clawlike, thinking, *Not yet! You ain't got Jess Hanna yet!*

CAA-RACK! The fore topmast went, riven to driftwood, clutters of rigging twitching behind it as it vanished in the lowering curtain. The deck was a rubbish heap of spars, canvas and lines. There were no sails, but the masts were there, swaying back and forth with a peculiar trembling, like giant chalk sticks tracing weird patterns on a vast blackboard.

Starr was everywhere, and seemingly all at once, his voice equally omnipresent. Now he was at the wheel struggling with 'Lisha; then across the flooded waist chasing after Meigs and Tavi and Abiel Cook as they thrashed through the wreckage; next on the foredeck yelling at Jess.

"Hanna! Help the Irisher with that staysail! Start, blast you!"

The fore topmast staysail was down on the deck, bunched and folded like a giant envelope against the starboard bulwarks. It was bloated and blistered and quivering like jelly with the ton of water it contained. Barnaby was trying to flatten it out with his body. Jess stumbled toward him with his knife and flopped. He stabbed repeatedly at the swollen sail, letting out the water.

Like a bomb bursting alongside them, a wave exploded over their heads and they went sweeping over the break in the foredeck and plunged into the swirling lake in the waist, Jess fetching up against the weatherboard in the galley doorway.

The cookhouse was a foot deep in flotsam-clotted water—seapig, saltpork, biscuits, crockery, hardware, pots and pans clattered and crashed and clanged over and over in a wild hurly-burly, rushing crazily from larboard to starboard, forward to aft, gurgling and bobbing in the inky backwash. Broken bottles and chopping knives and Lord knows what came tumbling over Jess. Struggling to his hands and knees he looked around and wondered how he would ever regain his station in the bows.

The stocky *Bunyan* was tottering before the vicious blows of the sea beast and reeling to her beam ends. The spume and spray were driving across her in sheets. The sea was beaten flat, yielding to the howling sky. But the old spouter would not yield. She righted gradually, heaving tons of water through her bow gunports and over her battered bulwarks—came to an even keel and plunged unsteadily, then swung her head downwind and raced away.

Jess waited until the bulk of the galley's wicked

mess had swept over the weatherboard and joined the greater churning wash on the deck, and then he sprang up and went plowing forward.

The jib was the only headsail left and it had torn loose from its clew and was streaming out like a tattered battle flag, flapping itself to shreds. Jess joined Barnaby and they started clawing at it, fighting it, and brought it down and secured it to the sheet and ran it up again. It puffed, billowed and snapped taut with the sharp crack of a rifle shot. It wouldn't hold for long, but every minute of headway was precious in the heaving turmoil.

The storm jib helped to give the whaler steerage way and to ease the pull of the wheel on 'Lisha Nook's racked arms. Starr hazing them, the crew staggered about, blinded by the flying spume and with the breath sucked from their lips before they could fully inhale it, doing what they could to hold the old bark together.

The *Bunyan* shuddered through the living darkness, rolling and plunging with the wind and wave force— the wind sweeping spitefully after her with a following sea, howling and screeching through her skeletal rigging.

And across the pseudo-darkness appeared a thick white line of foam as tall as a New Bedford barn. It seemed to gather a faint gleam of phosphorescent light from the sun that was completely obscured by the driving clouds, and it came at them with a hiss that turned into a roar. A running wild wall of water.

Jess glanced over his shoulder and saw that charging white rampart and knew it was hopeless. They were going to be caught by the screaming hill of water—pooped whether they liked it or not. He turned his streaming face to Barnaby and shouted.

"Watch out for yourself!"

He glanced aft again and saw the monster wave curling high over the stern and it looked as violent in aspect as a drooling madman running amok with an ax.

Jess didn't hesitate to consider the possibilities. Clutching up some slack in his lifeline in one hand, he grabbed the coaming with the other and vaulted over the break in the foredeck, dropping straight into the flooded waist.

His feet struck the slick deck and whipped out beneath him and he went headfirst into the swirling water, banging the breath from his lungs as he met the submerged deck—rolling, spewing, bringing his head up just as the wave struck the ship. Then he felt the reaction under him—the shuddering, flattening force as lumps of cold green water crashed over his head, smashing him back to the deck and into liquid amber darkness.

His last conscious thought was, *It's bad . . . so giddy awful bad . . . but it's not painful.*

He didn't think he had been out. Maybe for two or three seconds, but that was all. It was as if his mind had opened a shadowy door and wobbled into limbo

—turned quickly around and staggered out again, slamming the door behind.

So why not get your face out of water and try breathing some air again? his mind suggested.

He struggled to his hands and knees and hauled himself to his feet against the starboard bulwark. Something was moving out there on the mad sea—a tall black mass rolling helplessly in a complete loss of stability. It appeared to be a small ship, a schooner-rigged craft with an odd hull design. It went skittering off into the murk as a black wrack of spume-flung water hurtled by.

The *Bunyan* bucked into a swirling wall of sea, foam and mist, and the bowsprit pierced the low-pressure belt. She scudded into the windless eye of the storm. The waves going on around formed into willful leaping cones, twenty to thirty feet high, then collapsed abruptly, instantly reforming somewhere else.

This spot was the center of the depression, where the law regulating the strength of the wind proportions the difference of pressure between the place from which it comes and the place toward which it blows. A sort of typhoon clearing house.

Waves like mountains of gleaming black onyx piled up and crashed down on the whaler's deck. Thousands of invisible hands reached out and slapped her through the nightmare maze of high water. She shuddered and sprayed like a wet dog coming out of a pool, shaking itself from nose to tip of tail—and went skimming and careening along, as yet undefeated.

Jess gained the foredeck again, looking around for

Barnaby. There was no sign of the Irishman. That rag of storm jib was working loose and he started for it. It was the one thing that might keep the whaler before the wind.

Starr loomed before him, right out of the gusty darkness and whipping spume—majestic and soaking and swaying with the crazy pitch of the deck.

"Lay to the starboard cathead, Hanna! Get a line! The catblock's working loose!"

Mechanically, Jess turned to the right and lumbered toward the cathead. The monstrous iron-fluked anchor looked all right to him. He snatched up a fore topgallant halyard and leaned over the bow bulwark. What on earth was Starr talking about? There was nothing wrong with—

The hook caught under the back of his belt, and he realized in a flash of instinctive horror that he had stupidly let the mate trick him. He was being lifted bodily over the bulwark, without a chance to grab for support!

The black, rushing sea tilted under him, and he heard Starr's mocking voice.

"The dead go overside, my son!"

Jess crashed into liquid blackness, tons of it, all heavy and solid and moving. Then the weight seemed to lift and he lifted with it—up and up and up. And, surprisingly, there was air and he gulped at it and opened his eyes and saw the dark mass of the ship towering over him.

He tried to get a fingernail grip on that smooth black hull slipping by him, but he couldn't. There was nothing to get a hold on. And then a foaming sea poured between him and the ship and the next thing he knew he was clear of the stern and surrounded by howling darkness.

10. It Ain't Nice But It Can't Be Helped

UNABLE TO see or to time the waves, Jess tried frantically to time his breathing to coincide with his sudden rises to the surface, but there was so much flung spume in the air it was nearly impossible for him to tell when he was under and when he wasn't.

Fear ran amok in him. He was being swept away from the ship and into the rampaging Antarctic Ocean!

Water dragged like tearing hands at his clothes, stripping his shirt from his body. He gasped for air, trying to think what to do. But he couldn't think; he could only struggle in the rush and plunge of the swells. Sickeningly, he slid down into a trough of the sea, his stomach sloshing about like water in a canteen, and started up the other side. He saw the dark shape of a ship.

141

It was below him and it was mastless. The schooner-rigged craft he had seen earlier! It was an East Indies vessel, a *prau* or *palari*. But it might just as well have been a Black Ball Line clipper for all the help he could expect from her.

He went up—he went down; now out of sight of the wreck—again peering down at its decks from the crest of a watery hill. He was helpless. He had no will or strength of his own.

He was lifted and flung like a cork toward the tilted craft, dashed to within a foot of the shattered rail and sucked back. Then the sea heaved up and tumbled him head over heels across the strange deck in a wild welter of water.

He hit something hard and was rolled over it—all knocks and bangs and without breath—and then the bottom dropped out of everything and he shot straight down and crashed into water again. Incongruously, he was sitting in water up to his neck and he was breathing!

His wits swam together and he realized he had been tumbled into the hold of the *prau*. It was not a nice place to be. The inklike blackness made the hold a bedlam of bodiless sound. Shattered crates and stove casks were bumbling about in the crazy water; and something else—dead people.

Bloated corpses were tumbling about in the quaggy place—he could feel them pressing all around him!

The derelict shuttled crabwise and a heavy knock, a muted crash, sounded from up forward. The timbers shivered violently as if in the grip of an earthquake.

The *prau* sagged, biting deep into the water. A crate or cask, something hard, hit the back of his head. A corpse bobbled against his face. He pawed the loathsome thing away.

"This is no place to die in!" he cried, without thinking that the people around him were dead.

He struggled to his feet as the *prau* jerked around to starboard, rattling him and the dead, the casks and crates all together like marbles in a box. His outflung hand brushed down a wooden upright and he felt rungs. A ladder!

Thrashing through dead men and staves and bobbling casks, his primary thought was he mustn't panic; even as a great jumbled mass of cargo and corpses jammed him against the ladder he gripped this vital thought as though it were tangible.

He was pushed violently to one side of the ladder. Something banged his ear in the raucous dark. Something else wrapped around his submerged legs. He kicked it loose and reached up, felt a flat wooden step and began worming his way upward.

The open hatch showed fleeting glimpses of the sky wrack framed in a square of soft black. Water deluged on him in a solid block, trying to tear loose his handholds.

He struggled like an ant fighting its way through the gushing neck of a bottle funnel. He folded his wet body into the framework of the ladder and clung there doggedly as the heavy sheets of water broke over his head and shoulders. Painfully, he inched toward the open square that led to the sky.

He wrapped his hands around the hatch rim and, as the last wash of sea drained from his body, he hauled himself over the rough edge and flopped on the streaming deck.

Jess saw the sea—black gleaming tents of curling water reaching for the tattered waist of the *prau*. The deck tilted to larboard and disappeared completely under the running froth. As the wave hissed away, Jess came to his feet in a crouch and started for the only point of safety he could see. The *prau*'s high poopdeck in the stern.

He pulled himself out of the wrack and water in the waist and crawled across the slippery poopdeck. Thank God the hull of a *prau* was built to resemble her model —the old-fashioned Portuguese galleon of the sixteenth century—or he would have drowned on deck.

The deck was smooth, slanting toward the waist. There was no shelter on the poop, no helm to lash himself to. The spanker was gone, of course—overboard with the mainmast. Jess crawled on desperately. He reached the stumpy double-barred taffrail just as a high crackling wave rose over the stern.

The water fell on him like a mass of iron. He grasped the four-by-four bar of the taffrail in a loop of his arms, knitted his fingers together in a deathgrip and hung on.

The force of the water flattened him against the hardwood deck, twisted him like a rope's end and scraped him from one end of the bar to the other. The brackish liquid burned in his sinuses and filled his sight with shooting lights. He prayed.

Let the bar hold, God. Please let the bar hold!

The water drained across the slanted deck and spilled into the turmoil in the waist. Jess sat up and reached for a severed line that was coiled at his feet like a drowned snake. Its far end was secured to a ring bolt in the deck. He lashed it about his waist and prepared to wait.

In a moment of clear reasoning he saw how things were with him and the derelict *prau*. She was dismasted, her hull was flooded, and she was down in the water to her beam ends. It seemed to him that there had been an inordinate amount of empty casks in the cargo hold, and they were probably what kept her afloat.

So—as long as she didn't break up in the storm, the little poopdeck would remain above water level. It was the only speck of security he knew of in the black liquid world gone mad.

He closed his eyes and tried not to think of those drowned Indonesians washing around in the dark hold below.

Dawn cracked along the eastern horizon like a stage curtain rising slowly in a darkened theater.

Jess watched the first pale glints with sleepless eyes. Then he looked down at his wooden pallet. Nailheads pitted the deck. Despite putty calking, saltwater had seeped in and rusted brown splotches of rot on the planking. He patted the scarred surface with his hand.

Good old girl, he thought. *We rode her through.*

The sea was chopping up small lead-colored waves in an aimless fashion and the wind still blew, but fitfully now, like a continuous sigh of disappointment. The half-submerged *prau* wallowed restlessly in the crisp motion of the water.

Jess looked forward. Two feet of stumpy bows showed their snout above the nervous sea. The bowsprit was gone. The waist was monotonously awash —then bare; awash—then bare. The open and flooded cargo hatch glinted pink-gold like a morning tide pool.

He gazed along the golden border of the horizon, searching for a sail. There was nothing. Everywhere he looked was the sea—empty, forlorn. The enormity of his mid-ocean solitude settled on him and he shivered against the damp cold.

There would be no search made for him, directly or indirectly. The *Bunyan*'s crew would consider him lost overboard in the storm; and no one ever bothered about a missing native *prau*. They were never expected anywhere—coming and going on their mysterious errands as they had come and gone since the beginning of time, with no man pausing to wonder why or where or when. He cast another look at the expanding horizon, at the nothingness of dull contrasting colors. Then he sighed and sat up and began to untie himself from the ring bolt.

Well, he could simply roll over and die or he could go on fighting—hold out until his luck turned for the better. The *Bunyan* had taught him about fighting; how to cling tenaciously to life. Starr had not been able to break him, and now it was time to test his spirit against the elements.

Looking back it seemed to him that his life had been pretty soft, up until he was shanghaied. He had been a carefree, easygoing youth without purpose or aim or a spark of incentive. All right. Then he had seventeen years of shiftless living to make up for . . . if the *prau* would only hold together.

He stood up, every joint in his body stabbing pain messages to his brain. His stomach yawned hollow as he steadied himself on the slanted deck. A meal right now would be the thing.

What had Barnaby once told him—a man could live eight or nine days without any food or water?

Something like that. It was now dawn and the last time he had eaten was the morning before. Hmm. Eight or nine days. If he had water, he could prolong it.

Instantly his throat clogged. The demand was starting. He pictured his throat, the once tender passage now dry and wrinkled like used sandpaper, dustily scraping membrane against membrane. All his concentrated thought narrowed down to one pinpoint of urgency. Water.

He pawed at the salt cake on his crusty cheeks, thinking, *That won't get you anywhere. Stop tormenting yourself and do something about it.* But what?

The somber clouds of night turned a sullen gray as they faded into the background of the new day. The ocean expanded—vast, lonely, rolling inexorably away from one horizon on to the other.

He looked down at the cluttered maindeck. It was awash. A spar was caught between the rim of the hatch and a break in the starboard rail. A hand ax, its blade deep in the waterlogged wood, rode jauntily in the side of a cracked timber. Clots of rigging and nameless lines were tumbling across the waist in great tangles. The sea gurgled through the refuse, glittering silver in the weak sun.

Hopelessness rushed over him and he forgot his thirst. His lonely end seemed inescapable. The sea, the sky, the wrecked hulk—how could he hold out against these things?

And there was more—triangular fins caught his eye as they glided smoothly through the water, endlessly circling the wreck with dumb brute patience.

Jess hated the sharks with a childlike fury. He followed them with his eyes as they swerved gracefully toward the shattered rail. They acted as if they intended to fin aboard the flooded deck. Probably they knew about the dead men in the hold, and that was enough to tempt them into the colder southern waters.

"Don't you ever get enough?" Jess yelled at them. "Do you have to have me, too?"

He made up his mind to ignore them.

Climbing over the break in the poop, he stepped into the waist. The cold water hurried over his bare feet, enlarged them in its transparency, tinted them a pale orange. He waded across the afterdeck to the hatch and looked into a well of shimmering darkness.

It wasn't a job he wanted to do. He loathed it. But it had to be done before he became too weak to attempt it. He just might find something to eat or drink down there. Just might.

He untangled a long length of line and waded forward to secure one end to the antiquated windlass; the other end he lashed to his waist. Then he sloshed back to the hatch, faking down the line so that it would pay out freely.

He tried to construct the layout of the lower deck in his mind. The hold was amidships, of course, and aft of that there should be a compartment—a sort of cuddy or pantry.

All right. Turning, he grasped the rim of the hatch and lowered himself slowly into the water. He balked for a moment against the biting cold, balancing himself on the wooden edge.

"Go on. There must be food in the cuddy. Go on, you soger!"

He sucked a deep breath and dropped straight down.

It was murky. Objects appeared vague and bulky in the liquid half-light. He shoved a sluggish cask aside and straightened out to swim. Something loomed at him underwater and he put out his hand to ward it off. It was like clutching gelatin.

For a moment his mind refused to accept the message his hand was trying to communicate. He had to peer close into the goggle-eyed and gaping face before he could believe it. He shot back up through the hatchway, gasping for air.

"Belay that," he reasoned with himself. "It's only a dead man. What did you expect? It ain't nice, but it can't be helped. C'mon—let's try again."

He stalled. He wanted to look up at the sky, but he didn't. There was too much space, too much freedom there. It was too clean. He primed his lungs and let go.

Groping hurriedly through the maze of floating objects, he worked his way aft, telling himself, *That's a cask, that's a crate* . . . even thought his recoiling hands knew better. Then he was up against a crosswork of heavy timbers which separated the hold from the stern section, and he found an opening and shot through it and the bulkhead with the cuddy door rushed out of the gloom to meet him.

He fumbled with the latch. Nothing happened. It was locked!

He wrenched at the latch. Waste of time. He explored

the face of the door with trembling hands. It was solid, unyielding, probably teak.

Sick with discouragement, he backfinned, turning away. He had to leave. His lungs were starting to bulge in the back of his throat. Catching up the lifeline, he followed it out of the deep shadows and into the brighter water in the hold.

He was nosing up toward the hatchway when the line suddenly pulled taut—stopping him with a jolt!

He lunged forward, upward, jerking at the line. bobbing like a balloon on a string. The silver surface of the sea shimmered in the pale sun—only one foot above his upturned face.

His hands reached through the water and clutched at the nothingness of air. He could feel the breeze on his wet palms, but he couldn't get to it!

Don't struggle! You're lost if you struggle! Go back and find the hitch. Go back go back . . .

His lungs throbbing like Malay drums, a smear of brilliant specks glazing his blurred sight, he turned and hand-fumbled back along the lifeline. It drew him to the deck. The line was fouled between two water-logged crates. He shoved the first one aside, but the second one wouldn't budge. It was wedged in a knee joint.

He lunged himself against the crate. It shifted slug-gishly and he snapped the line clear. He swung away groggily, his head seemingly swelling like the bladder in a dead whale, and shot up into the silvered circle of the sun.

For the remainder of the day he sat disconsolately on the poopdeck and watched the gray sea. In the early evening, when the sun began its slow drag down to the water and the encircling horizon started to tighten its boundaries, he lowered his head and closed his eyes.

He didn't want to see it; didn't want the night to close him in again with its cold and its fears and its loneliness.

He relashed himself to the ring bolt and curled against the stubby taffrail. All he had for cover was a piece of damp sailcloth. His soul-sick gaze happened over the stern and he saw the triangular fins sliding effortlessly after the drifting wreck.

The sharks were still waiting.

11. How Many Miles To Antarctica?

DAWN FOUND him hunched on the deck in a seizure of cold and hunger cramps. He groaned, his knees drawn up to his chest, realizing that he would have to try the hold again. Breaking into the cuddy seemed to be his only answer.

At midmorning, when there was a faint warmth from the pallid sun, he waded back to the flooded hatch with the hand ax.

It was futile. The pressure of the water, his own shaky weakness, destroyed any dream of battering down the cuddy door. In desperation, he turned to the hold and rummaged blindly for anything that came to hand. He left with a soggy blanket and a dripping lantern. The hunger pains were beginning again.

He burst to the surface gasping with cramp, caught the rim of the hatch and hung there with his face pressed hard against the wood. Every so often a foamy trill of water would pour over his head. Finally, spent and trembling, he looked up.

Far across the dark blue water the sketchy outline of a tall sail was vanishing in the coppery sky of the west.

He cried out. He jacked himself out of the hold and stumbled across the flooded deck, waving the hatchet like a stiff banner. He went as far as he could—to the taffrail—then a shout died on his lips. The sail was sinking over the curvature of the earth. In a moment the sea was empty again.

For a good hour he wallowed in despondency and self-pity. He walked the poop, across the maindeck, up to the lifting bows and back again, like a captured jungle cat pacing its cage. Abstractly, his mind started to wander . . . .

The water was colder. He was drifting south. Did the old *prau* mean to take him to the South Pole? He tripped over the wedged spar in the waist and chuckled. He was a little crazy.

How far to the South Pole? How many weeks will it take? How many miles to Antarctica? His future looked very barren. He could starve or freeze to death. For a moment he contemplated suicide. But his will to survive, to live, revolted. His recent experience in the water had taught him that he could not voluntarily drown himself; and when it came to feeding himself to a shark . . . .

There was only one fin in the water now, leading the *prau* off the starboard bow. The southern waters must have grown too cold for the others.

"That's the spirit, Abijah!" Jess yelled at the shark. "Hang on, old fish! Never say die!"

Some of his confidence eked back. There might be other ships—a sealer or a whaler or a Crown cruiser. He had to hold out. And he had to be ready.

He fashioned a crude sort of grappling iron with a line, a block and a three-foot splinter of wood, and dragged the bottom of the hold with this device and hauled up three bodies. It was ghastly work but necessary. He searched the clothes on the bloated corpses until he found a priceless treasure. A tinderbox.

He opened the little box and removed the charred strip of linen and laid it on the poopdeck with the blanket to dry. Then he looked at the three bodies.

Cannibalism is not an inherent compulsion in human beings. Jess's cavemen ancestors did not eat each other. It was a custom started by latter-day savages for purely magical or ritualistic reasons. Some white men, seamen especially, did resort to it out of grim necessity; the survivors of the ill-fated *Essex* were a case in point, so Barnaby had said. But it wasn't for Jess.

Nor could he bring himself to feed the bodies to the shark he had dubbed Abijah—which would have been a simple means of disposing of them. Instead, he stuffed them back in the hold, up under the deck carlings, and hoped they would stay there.

He chopped down the taffrail and splintered it into

kindling. There was oil in the lantern and that would insure a conflagration. The next time a ship appeared in the offing he would be ready for it. It might mean burning the deck out from under him, but at least they would see it. *They would have to see it.*

He drank some of the oil from the lantern, hoping it would give him strength. It tasted briny and ghastly, but he got it down. Then he returned to the waist for more wood. It would take time to dry and every minute was suddenly very precious to him.

He unwedged the spar and propped one end on the edge of the poop and started to chop. In his fanatical haste he neglected to observe that the *prau* was foundering under a running sea.

The water washed up to the break in the poop, splashed over his supporting hand on the spar. He realized with a start that he was standing up to his waist in the sea.

Something coarse and hard brushed against the back of his submerged legs—muscular and living.

He spun about with a cry and slashed at the water with the hatchet. The shark, startled by the blow that barely grazed him, rolled over like an elongated barrel and his tooth-jaggy mouth snapped in the water. Jess struck again.

The shark tail-hitched toward the broken larboard rail. Jess thrashed after him, chopping the water white with the hatchet, but Abijah darted out of the hole and disappeared in the blue-gray depths.

Jess rocked weakly, holding his unsure balance against the wash of the incoming sea. The shark could

have saved him. The blood or lymph juices alone . . . .
His throat pinched and he cleared it painfully. He
looked down at the water rushing about his waist,
hating the salt that was in it.

The *prau* sagged with a roll of the sea. He was
thrown from his feet and went under and almost
plunged out through the hole in the rail. In the slate-
gray blur of water the jagged black wood of the rail
came at him and he grabbed for it, dropping the
hatchet. He shoved up, balancing precariously on the
rail, his head free of the water.

Was the *prau* breaking up? He had no way of knowing. All he could think of was to get back to the poopdeck. That narrow slab of wood was his symbol of
security.

He turned and began wade-swimming aft, struggling
against the current that was trying to sweep him out
into the vast open sea. A fin suddenly appeared, sliding evenly through the yeasty water in the waist. Abijah was back—just as if he knew that Jess was no
longer armed!

Jess's feet sank to the deck and he stood up, bracing
himself as he watched the triangular danger sign
curve away from the break in the poop. With a touch
of panic he realized he was cut off from the afterdeck.

Total fear captured him and he thrashed about
and started forward, half wading, half swimming. His
leadened feet struck the rim of the hatch and he
stepped off into the hold.

He thought he was lost and he cried out under water.

Then he started fighting again. He surged to the surface and began slapping it frantically with his palms, hoping to frighten off Abijah. He had only twenty feet of deck to cross to reach the bows, but it seemed like twenty miles. His stomach felt wide open and vulnerable and it rippled with nervous fear. He was certain Abijah was right behind him.

How many miles to safety, his fear-crazed mind asked.

He plunged through the water and into the bows, scrambled up on the stumpy remains of the bowsprit and straddled it, panting and choking. As the sea washed across the maindeck the water sloshed over his buttocks and his feet sank into the cold liquid. The taper-bodied blue-gray shark tail-kicked toward him.

Jess winced, holding his breath for the sea to subside, for the bow to lift again. *Hurry,* he thought. *Hurry!*

But Abijah was out of his element in the confines of the narrow bows. He had no room to curve and snap. His saucerlike myopic eyes studied Jess stupidly. Abruptly, in a flurry of foam, he was gone.

Jess was near sobbing. His throat was burning fire and a needle of pain hemstitched rhythmically across his stomach. He couldn't hope to hold on to that unsteady seesaw perch for long. He was too weak. He would fall off. Abijah would get him eventually.

Why didn't the sea settle and give the *prau* a chance? How much longer could she hold together? He released a clutched hand and rubbed at his face, trying vainly to wipe away the cobwebs of fatigue. He would have to get back to the poopdeck, that was all; have to chance the shark.

But he didn't. He stayed where he was and held on. He waited.

Night edged down the pale sky and the copper rim of the west glimmered and closed shut. The darkened sea ran to him, sparkling with phosphorescence. Silver motes formed under the bows and poured a protozoic treasure into the fiery water. Soon the wreck was drifting in a carpet of brilliant color.

Jess's heavy, burning eyes stared blankly around. A fairyland of terror, he thought, and his head nodded down. Sleep . . . how comforting and secure was sleep . . . .

He jerked up his head a moment later. His legs had slipped into the water to his knees. He retrieved them and sat hunched and shivering like a sick parrot on its perch.

Don't fall asleep, he warned himself. *You must stay awake.*

A sigh echoed across the immeasurable ocean; to the east, the sharp *plop-ploop* sound of fish striking water. Feeding time, Jess thought. The hunger cramps were gone now, but that didn't give him much solace. He knew that once they had passed, his body and soul were on the downhill road.

A new sound cracked out of the night to add one more stone to his pyramid of misery—an insistent creaking from the *prau*'s waterlogged timbers. *She'll break up soon,* he thought. *Maybe she won't make it through the night.* If the sea would only settle . . .

Suddenly something enormous towered out of the sea on the starboard. Black, vague, glinting with phosphorescence at its base, it was like the resurrection of a long-sunken frigate. Water plashed from its luminous sides and Jess heard a gusty wheeze. It sank again, like a barely audible sigh.

Jess shivered and looked at the flooded maindeck. The running sea had flattened to a black oily ripple. *Can you do it now,* he wondered. *Now, before it's too late? The poopdeck is back there. Safety. And the blanket. Warmth.*

He slipped off the butt of the bowsprit and into the water. It gurgled a few inches below his knees.

Stand by, Abijah. Here I come. He waded aft.

But Abijah was gone. Jess had the deck to himself. He splashed back to the break in the poop and pulled himself onto the dry deck. His kindling was still there, and the lantern and tinderbox were secure. He curled into a ball and drew the damp blanket over his trembling body. It was like coming home.

He dreamed he was in Lubber Land, that wonderful shore resort known as Fiddlers' Green, the sailors' paradise where there were pretty girls and music and dancing and tables loaded with food . . . .

His groggy mind swam wearily out of the heavy folds of a muddy brown sleep, his stomach rumbling like a gaseous volcano and his body grabbing with pain when he moved. Then he was awake.

I can't hold out, was his first thought. *Can't make it through another day.* Then the active part of his mind asked a question: *What woke you up?*

He pulled himself into a sitting position and opened his eyes. A heavy mist or near fog lay over the face of the night like a gray curtain undulating quietly in a soft breeze. He listened, wondering, and then heard it—the long dismal *mmoooaah* of a foghorn or conch shell. He whipped the blanket aside and came to his knees.

Was it possible? Had he really heard it, or was it only a manifestation of his weakened condition? Had the old *prau* inadvertently drifted across the path of another ship? He knelt by the starboard rail, straining his eyes and ears against the blind mist. But there was nothing to see or hear. Yet he had heard it! He believed that; had to believe it.

"Come on, mate. Blow again. Show yourself!"

He waited with the shakes, clutching at the rail, and still there was nothing. He lowered his head. It was a rotten trick. It shouldn't happen to a dog. The three days of privation were telling on him now, and he slowly crumpled under the weight of hunger and exposure. He lay with his face pressed to the moist blanket and he started to sob. It was time to slip his cable, to roll over and quietly die.

Mmmooooaah! Again the throaty bass voice droned through the mist. Jess raised his head. A ship was sounding for icebergs by listening to the rebound of the horn's echoes. There was no mistaking the sound. He struggled to his knees again, gasping with exertion, and fumbled with the lantern, spilling the oil over the kindling pile.

Why did the night have to be misty? They could have seen his fire so easily on a clear night. He struck a spark with the flint and steel, but that was all he achieved—one quick bright pinpoint spark. The charred strip of linen was still damp.

Jess gawked at the worthless tinderbox and struck again.

"No!" he cried. "Don't let this happen!"

He struck and struck and struck—spark spark spark, but no flame.

MMMOOOAAH! The conch shell seemed to go off in his head. He looked up with a start and saw the black prow of a vessel slicing through the wet curtain of mist. It was a topsail schooner and it towered majestically above the wrecked *prau*. It was going to catch the wreck smack amidships!

Jess started to yell, his throat feeling as though it were ribbed with knifeblades—

"Derelict ahead! *Hard a-larboard!*"

There was a startled yelp from someone in the bows, and then a string of frantic shouting as booted feet went thumping across the deck. Jess stood up as the looming schooner began to pay off to larboard, but he could see she wasn't going to clear in time. Collision was inevitable. He started to turn, to run . . . .

The deck leaped from under his feet and he felt a gigantic power pitch him away from the *prau* and into a deep belt of blackness. For a split moment he was conscious only of noise—clashing, grinding, all-powerful. It packed all physical sensation into his upper chest and he opened his mouth to scream.

He hit the water hard, head and back, and still the noise, muted and throbbing, pushed at him, pressurized him into a twirling ball of helplessness. Light broke through darkness. A hazy red wall advanced and retreated with waverings and flutterings of color. And then blackness, total and final.

It was unbelievable that it was happening, that he was actually sinking into the center of a black liquid void, that his eighteen years of life were suddenly, senselessly over. And just when he had been at the point of rescue!

He couldn't settle for it. He twisted blindly around and started clawing his way to the surface. But it was so far off, so very very far off . . . .

He didn't really come completely around. A part of his mind stayed down below in the black icy water. He was aware of hands under his armpits, and he heard the water plashing from his body as the hands lifted him, and he felt the rasp of a gunwale on his back as they pulled him over the side and into a dory. But none of it seemed to matter. He saw no reason for all this fuss. He was even a little annoyed with the strangers. Why didn't they give him his blanket and let him go back to sleep?

Instead of that they pawed him and hammered him with voices. He could hear what they were saying— could even understand some of it—but none of it really had any bearing. Silly, useless questions: What was he doing out there? Was he alone? What ship was that they had rammed? How long had he been drifting?

And then one voice, high-pitched with excitement, cut through the others—"Where did you think you were going, mate? To the South Pole?"

And something clicked in Jess's brain.

"How many miles to Antarctica?" he asked, and he smiled and lay back in the warm security of the weedy meadow that belonged in another land at another time.

12. Mutiny's the Word

THEY PUT Jess in the mate's compartment and buried him in a mound of coarse warm blankets, and poured whisky-laced coffee down him, and then hot soup, until finally he was ready to sit up and go to work on a bowl of stew.

He was on the American sealing schooner *Gay Squall*. The skipper, a smiling man in his mid-twenties, was named Aquilla Giffords and he was from Norwich, Connecticut, where uncommon names were common. He paid Jess a visit as the ravenous youth was putting in the final licks on his stew and wondering how soon he might expect to receive the next bowl.

"I owe you my thanks," Captain Giffords said, making himself a seat on the mate's seachest. "If you hadn't

166

sung out when you did we would have rammed bow-
on with that derelict. As it was the helmsman managed to bring us about just enough to get off with a
sprained hull. We're recalking the sprung seams now."

He paused and gave Jess an inquiring smile.

"Every man jack, including me, is wondering what
in grab's name you were doing away out here aboard
that wreck?"

"Just blind luck," Jess said. "I was shoved overside
by the first mate in a typhoon."

"Did you say *shoved?*"

"Aye, sir, that's the word. Just like murdered."

Captain Giffords cocked an ironic eye.

"I think you best tell me about it."

In shortened form Jess told the young skipper the
story of his *Bunyan* misadventures—starting with the
clandestine meeting in the Commodore Mayo's barn,
and working step by step up to Mr. Ralls's mysterious
death, and ending at the time when Starr caught him
off guard and threw him over the side and—as he
put it—he blundered upon the derelict by sheer blind
luck.

Jess came to a full stop and young Giffords pursed
his mouth and said *Huh!* Then he said:

"That's some yarn. And I reckon it will wash. I've
heard of the *Bunyan* afore. Bad-luck ship, so they say.
And I've heard of Starr, too. A mean bucko. Strange
thing is—we spoke the *Bunyan* only two days ago."

"You did? Where was that?"

"Here in the Current. She had taken a brutal maul-
ing in that typhoon and was limping in to Macquarie

Island to make repairs—so they said. She'd lost her foremast, and there was hardly enough left on her main to mount a jury rig. Seemed mighty under-manned, too, for a whaler."

"Aye," Jess muttered absently, "Starr's let her crew whittle down to a handful." He looked at Giffords. "Where is this Macquarie, Captain?"

"Midway between the southern tip of New Zealand and the Balleny Islands off the coast of Antarctica. It's good seal-hunting ground. We just finished putting in a profitable month there. 'Fact, we were only one day out when we crossed the *Bunyan*."

Jess thought for a moment—then said, "Captain, you said you owed me thanks for saving your schooner. Well, on the same score, you saved my life and I guess that makes us even. But I'm wondering if you'd do me a favor—like putting back to Macquarie?"

Giffords pulled a mild frown over his face.

"Why concern yourself any further about the *Bunyan*, Hanna? You're safe now, and good riddance to her, I'd say. I can always use a spare hand."

Jess shook his head. "It's something I've got to do, sir. Or at least *try* to do. I—well, I guess I can't put it in words, except to say that if I quit now—if I stay with you and become a sealer—then George Starr has whipped me." He paused, thinking about it.

"No," he said, "it's more than that. Starr and Gant mean to lose the *Bunyan* in the pack ice. I'm certain of it! And that means Captain Coffin and what's left of the crew will be lost too. You see? I can't just sit here, knowing that, and do nothing. Can I?"

Giffords's frown deepened until he looked nearly twice his age. "No," he said thoughtfully, "I suppose not." Then he straightened up on the seachest and said, "Look, Hanna. I can sympathize with your position and the lives of the *Bunyan*'s crew. But I don't own this schooner. I'm only a hired skipper, and I can't place my owner's vessel and crew in jeopardy. If she was my ship, I might help you do something about the *Bunyan*.

"I'm not asking you to," Jess said. "All I want is to be set down on Macquarie so I can get back to my ship. That's not much, is it? Say you lose a week. You'd have lost a lot more if you had stove in your bow on that derelict."

Giffords grunted and nodded. "There's something in that," he agreed. "All right. I think you're a tomfool to stick your neck back in Starr's bowline—but if that's what you want—"

"Aye," Jess said doggedly, "it's what I want."

The *Gay Squall* raised Macquarie on the third day. It was an isolated turtle-backed island covered with grassy vegetation and with stumpy trees and shrubs in the sheltered sections. There were several anchorages but no harbors. Great clusters of penguins pegged the shore-bound rocks and a busy cloud of seafowl wheeled over the westernmost bay. A huge herd of sea elephants began a raucous outcry as the schooner put into a rock-ribbed cove.

Jess and Giffords went ashore in a dory and threaded their way through the lackadaisical sea elephants who made no motion toward self-preservation other than to bellow and roar and flap their flippers in vexation. Bewildered, Jess looked around at the great herd.

"Why did you leave here? Looks like you could find enough oil and fur on this beach to fill a dozen schooners."

Giffords placed a foot on a lichenous rock and stared at a fat long-nosed old gentleman who was bellowing his outrage at them.

"This island," he said, "was discovered only twelve years ago. At that time you could hardly see the place for seals. Now look at 'em. Already only a few herds left. I tell you, Hanna, if we sealers keep on at this rate we'll exterminate the entire seal family." He shrugged. "My policy is to take a little, leave a little. There's always another day."

"Aye," Jess agreed. "And the same goes for whalers. The way we're going now, I guess there will come a day when the whale will be—uh—"

"Extinct," Giffords said. "Gone from the face of the sea. Vanished forever." He removed his foot from the mossy rock. "C'mon," he said in a soft voice.

They went on up over one of the grassy brows of the submarine mountain and looked down into the next bay. It was just sunset and the nearly dismasted *Bunyan* was squatting in the ice-checkered ebb waters of a shallow anchorage.

"There she blows," Giffords said.

Jess, mute, nodded. Finding the *Bunyan* was somewhat like stumbling upon the materialization of a vague dream—or nightmare. The enigmatic mystery of the ship brushed him with a peculiar uneasiness, and a sense of moral disturbance that he couldn't understand settled on him like an indescribable malaise.

"Aye," he murmured.

Giffords reached under his jacket and drew out a boarding pistol and handed it to Jess.

"I think you'll likely need that," he said.

They went back down to the sea elephant cove and climbed into the dory. Giffords's manner was reserved and reflective, and halfway to the schooner he turned to Jess.

"You're a blasted fool, Hanna. But if you're determined to get yourself killed, then you'll need this dory to get out to the *Bunyan*."

Jess found the young captain's hand in the dark.

"Thanks," he said. "Thanks for everything."

The dory pulled alongside the schooner and Giffords's boatcrew went up the side.

"Good luck, Hanna," Giffords said. "Maybe we'll meet up some day along the Atlantic coast."

"I'll look forward to it," Jess said and reached for the oars.

Giffords paused at the gangway, staring down at the whalerman.

"I hate to let you go this way," he said. "I wish I could . . . ."

Whatever he wished was never known. Jess fended off from the schooner's side with his larboard oar, calling back, "Greasy luck, *Gay Squall!*" Then he was absorbed in the night.

He rowed stubbornly around the butt end of the rocky headland and into the other bay. The *Bunyan*, looking as squat as a floating whale, sat stolidly in the frosty star-shot waters. Jess rowed over to the starboard and rested on the oars, studying the shadowy deck. There didn't appear to be any watch.

He pulled under the bowsprit and secured the dory to the lower bobstay. Then, grasping the upper stay in both hands, he raised himself to the billethead and climbed in over the bows.

He froze at the starboard cathead, searching the deck with his eyes, then started aft along the fancy rail to the fore-shrouds. The foremast, he saw, had lost its topmast and topgallant. It stood up from the

deck like a fat bare flagpole. The mainmast had lost
its topgallant and most of its tophamper. He couldn't
see that any work or repairs had been done aloft.

He slipped down to the fore-companionway. A ven-
eer of ice had formed on the spar deck and it crunched
crisply under his feet. He opened one of the doors and
looked down into a smoky sickly yellow light. A
grumble of voices murmured below. Everything
seemed all right. Jess started down the steps.

There were five men in the fo'c'sle. They were
hunched over the mess table talking in low urgent
tones, with the carling lamp smoking sulfurously over
their heads. When they looked up and saw Jess standing in the gloom of the companionway they reacted

like children who had been frightening each other with ghost stories and had suddenly been visited by a manifestation of one.

'Lisha Nook actually screamed. Return Meigs jumped to his feet as if to run—somewhere. Jehiel Galpin's mouth dropped open and he was struck speechless and immobile, and Tavi—deeply steeped in Polynesian superstition—covered his eyes as if to ward off the sight of an evil spirit. Barnaby was the only one who found his voice.

"Faith! Is it yerself, lad? Is it me darlin Jess or 'tis it his ghost I'm seeing?"

Return Meigs's right hand edged toward a boat hatchet stuck in the side of the pawl-post. Jess grinned at him.

"Avast that, Meigs," he said. "An ax will go right through a ghost—but it would stove me proper."

"Saints presarve us!" Barnaby cried. "He speaks! By all that's holy and wonderful it *is* me darlin bhoy! And it's alive he is!"

"Alive and kicking," Jess said. He came down the last of the steps to the stern of the table. "Will no man offer a cold shipmate a cup of java on a freezing night?"

They mobbed him then—laughing, pawing him, all talking at once. And Tavi cautiously uncovered his eyes and risked a second look at the "dead man" who had returned from his watery grave.

"You fella Jess," he said disbelievingly, "body belong you walkabout altogether?"

"Aye Tavi. Body and spirit I've come aboard altogether."

Barnaby was pounding Jess excitedly on the back.

"What happened to yez, lad? Sure and we all said the darlin boy-o has been deep-sixed in the typhoon, he has that. By the holies, ye must carry St. Christopher himself in yer pocket!"

"It could be," Jess said. "But it was no saint that paid me off by the boom. This isn't a Tom Pepper yarn—it's cold fact."

He told them about Starr and the wrecked *prau* and the *Gay Squall* and how Captain Giffords had helped him; and as the whalermen listened to his remarkable story, their sea-grained faces hardened with a look of malevolence that Jess had never seen in them before.

The truth was, they had just about reached the end of their tether with Starr and the *Bunyan*. They were so depleted as a crew that they could man only one whaleboat if the need arose; the ship was now a near wreck, and Starr had passed no orders to make repairs; and they were slowly coming to suspect that they had been led down into the deadly Antarctic for some sinister purpose that could only bring them further misfortune.

They were not imaginative men; a dumb acceptance of disciplined toil was what made their mental capstans go round. But enough inexplicable things had happened aboard the *Bunyan* during her year at sea to create a questioning suspicion in even a brute mind. And now Jess was standing before them and telling them that Starr had attempted to murder him.

"Why?" Jehiel Galpin asked.

"Because I was a threat to him," Jess said. "I knew too much. Mr. Ralls knew too much, and look what happened to him. I tell you Starr intends to lose this ship for her insurance. And he'll lose all of you with her. He tried to do it on the *Bunyan*'s last voyage, but Mr. Ralls managed to save her. It was all planned out by Starr, Mr. Munro and Jack Hay before we sailed."

"But if Hay was in on it, why did somebody go and slip his cable on him?" Galpin wondered.

"I don't know," Jess said. "I've never been able to fathom that." He made an impatient gesture and said, "But that doesn't matter now. What counts is—what are we going to do about it? Are we just going to stand around like a stupid row of belaying pins and let Starr and Gant kill us all?"

"Be cursed if we will!" Barnaby cried. "It's sick I am of this rum business and of Starr's blows. What say, me boy-os? We'll take the ship, eh?"

Jehiel Galpin leaned over the table, his narrow face tense and expectant and almost demoniac in the sickly timber-light.

"It's mutiny then?" he whispered raspingly.

"Aye! Mutiny's the word," Return Meigs growled He snatched the boat hatchet from the pawl-post.

Tavi, as taciturn as ever, went away soundlessly and returned a minute latter carrying an eight-foot lance and a narrow-bladed razor-edged boat spade. Barnaby reached for the spade with a flashing grin.

"All hands for cutting in!" he crowed. "We've weapons enough for the likes of Starr's blubber!"

"Aye," Jess said and drew the pistol young Giffords had given him. "And we have this. C'mon. Let's get it over with."

As heavily armed as a crew of barbaric corsairs, they trooped up the companionway. In their excitement and anger not one of them noticed that 'Lisha Nook was missing.

13. Come Aboard, Mr. Hanna

A GREAT SIFTING of glazed stars swung over their hunched heads as they started aft. The film of frost crunched under their feet as they slipped across the cold deck. They passed through the black shadow pool under the forward boatrack and split up to go around the tryworks, fanning out when they reached the waist.

Jess stopped short, staring ahead. Something was out of place on the afterdeck—or rather, something that didn't belong there was in place. He looked around hurriedly and whispered:

"Where's 'Lisha?"

"Dunno," Jehiel grunted.

POW! A pistol cracked on the afterdeck and Starr's voice roared in the splintered slience. "Pour it to 'em!"

"At 'em all hands!" Jess yelled, and he fired his pistol pointblank as the mutineers broke into a flat-footed charge across the crisping deck.

A crackle of shots blazed from the afterdeck and Jehiel Galpin went *Uuuah* and doubled over in his run, taking one two three more fast steps forward, lost his balance and crashed headlong into the well pump.

Jess and Tavi reached the shadow-black band under the waist boatrack together, and Jess saw that a hastily constructed barricade of boxes and mattresses had been piled just afore the two little stern houses and the skylight, and saw that Starr, Gant, the two harpooners and 'Lisha Nook were crouching behind it with a bristling array of boarding pistols and muskets.

Caught in an ambush! Nook had betrayed them! Jess spun about, taking a wild grab at Tavi, yelling, "Back! Get back!"

Three guns spurted bright orange flame over the barricade and somebody cried out in the waist as Tavi, a tall sleek Herculean silhouette in the starlight, slid to a halt with the lance poised over his right shoulder, threw his left arm straight out for balance and cast the eight-foot dart.

The lance went *www-it* in the crisp air and caught 'Lisha Nook smack in the chest and rammed him wham against the larboard house and held him pinned to the bulkhead, and he started to scream and thrash his arms and tried to do something about that ghastly pole in his chest, but it was too late. He was dead.

Jess ran back across the waist with bullets snicking on ahead of him, and spotted someone down on one

knee on the deck just abaft the tryworks, and caught
the man under the armpit and jerked him to his feet,
saw that it was Barnaby, and together they trundled
around the protective corner where Barnaby slumped
to the deck with a long groan.

"Me fut!" he gasped. "I've a devil's bullet in me
giddy fut, I have so!"

Tavi and Return Meigs rushed behind the brick
tryworks and hunkered down to get their breath. Starr's
voice ragged at them from the sheltered afterdeck.

"Splice me! Do 'ee call that a mutiny, you batchy
scum! Come aft with your complaints, my sons, and
I'll doctor you again!"

"Waiting for us!" Meigs growled, outraged with
frustration. "That scurvy seaslug 'Lisha Nook! We
should a remembered he's always toadied up to Starr.
Why didn't *somebody* think to look for him afore we
attacked?

"Stow that," Jess snapped. "Tavi took care of 'Lisha.
Barnaby's hurt. Help him below and see what you can
do for his foot. Tavi and me'll stay here. Starr's bunch
won't dare come forward now they know we have a
pistol."

"A precious lot of good it'll do us!" Meigs cried.
"They got all the firearms and food and water—"

From his sitting position, Barnaby's left fist shot
out and smacked Meigs's mouth, rocking the hunker-
ing seaman off his heels and onto his backside.

"Didn't ye hear Hanna, mate?" Barnaby demanded.
"Pipe down he said. Give uz a hand now."

Distractedly, Jess watched the two seamen limp forward and vanish down the companionway. Tavi, armed now with a flensing spade and as stoical and unmoved as a wooden idol, watched the shadow-hid afterdeck over the top shelf of the tryworks.

Jess glanced at the Polynesian with admiration and awe. That was an amazing cast Tavi had made with the heavy lance. Must have been all of thirty feet. And smack in the chest . . . Hm. Reminded him of something else . . . But he was too plagued with anxiety to think about it.

He and his three shipmates were in a bad fix. Meigs had been right; Starr didn't have to attack them. He could just sit back and starve them out. And there didn't seem to be a thing Jess and the others could do about it. Barnaby was now useless, and Jess and Tavi and Meigs would be slaughtered if they attempted another attack across the deck. So—

A sudden raucous cry rang out from the fo'c'sle, and Tavi glanced over his shoulder with an incurious look.

"Return must be doctoring Barnaby," Jess said. He walked over to the open companionway and went half-way down the steps.

Barnaby was on his back on the mess table with the carling lamp ablaze in his face, and Return Meigs was bending over the Irishman's bare bloody left foot with his thick-bladed sheath knife in his hand. Barnaby's moony face had that peculiar ashen tint that heavily tanned men always get when they undergo severe pain.

Meigs looked up at Jess with a pleased grin.

"Took a bit of calking, but I got it." He held a small lead-gray pellet up to the light.

"Lord A'mighty, Meigs!" Jess cried. "Why didn't you use a blubber spade? Then you could of taken off his *whole* foot?"

Meigs looked crestfallen.

"Well, my knife was the only tool at hand," he muttered.

Barnaby groaned and made a feeble gesture with his hand.

"Was it only his knife then?" he asked weakly. "Sure and it felt like a belaying pin with a marlin spike lashed to the end, it did that. Return, ye darlin man, will ye be stepping aft here a foot or two—just enough so's I can get me hands on yer scrawny throat! I'll be after *Returning* you!"

"Here's the thanks a man gets for fishing a bullet out of a wounded shipmate!" Meigs said vexatiously —but taking pains to stay well afore Barnaby's huge clutching hands.

"Belay that," Jess said. "Lash up Barnaby's foot with some linen and come on deck. I've got a plan."

"Well, let's hope it's a cable's length better than your last one," Meigs said spitefully. "Else we'll *all* have lead ballast in our hulls!"

Jess ignored Meigs's blunt thrust and returned to the deck. Tavi was still stolidly standing his post behind the tryworks. Five minutes later Return Meigs joined them.

"Listen," Jess began. "We can't just sit here like

frozen pelicans till they starve us out. So my idea is to catch them offguard. We'll attack—"

"*Attack!*" Meigs wailed. "Slip my wind, Hanna, they'll cut us into horse pieces if we try that tomfoollery again!"

"I don't mean across the deck," Jess said. "The *Gay Squall's* dory is still lashed to the bobstay under the bows. Tavi and I will slip into it and pull around to the stern. Then we'll climb up to the alleyway roof and we'll have Starr in a box from above and behind. Either they disarm themselves when I give the word, or I'll shoot Starr dead."

Meigs grunted, thinking about it.
"What's my course while you two board ho?"

"You stay here and hold the foredeck. If they try to make a break to come forward, you'll have to stop 'em with the weapons on hand. You can handle a lance, can't you?"

"Aye," Meigs grumbled. "But I can't handle *four men with one lance!*"

"I can promise you there won't be four," Jess said. "If anybody tries to break, it will only be the two harpooners. Because Tavi and I will take care of Starr and Gant. And then we'll be right behind Munson and Burr with our hatchets. See?"

"Aye, Meigs said dubiously. "It *might* work.

"*Has* to work," Jess said. "It's our only out. Any other course and we're dead men."

It was midnight. There was no moon—only the heavy sprinkle of frosted stars. Jess and Tavi armed themselves; Jess shoving the pistol in the front of his belt and a boat hatchet in the back, and Tavi taking only two hatchets (all male Kanakas of that period were uncommonly handy at throwing tomahawks). Jess slapped Meigs on the shoulder.

"Remember what Captain Lawrence said when he was dying aboard the *Chesapeake*. 'Don't give up the ship.'"

Return Meigs fumbled for Jess's hand in the dark.

"Greasy luck, shipmate," he muttered, and turned to Tavi. "Fella hatchet belong you walkabout altogether, Tavi."

The Kanaka gave a terse grunt and went forward hunched over. Jess followed him. The jibboom and martingale had been carried away in the typhoon, but the two seamen had no trouble scrambling down the bowsprit and the trailboard by way of the bobstays. The little dory was snuggling cozily against the cutwater like a baby at its mother's breast.

Jess and Tavi lowered themselves into the boat and cast off. They didn't use the oars, but hugged the whaler's leeward side and pulled themselves aft by using the flat of their hands against the chill side of the hull. Huge platelike slabs of gray-white ice drifted in the black water around the ship.

Jess and Tavi slipped under the starboard fore-chains, passed along the midships bulwark, and then beneath the mizzen channels and the convex buttock of the hull and swung around under the counter. The square sheer pitch of the boxed stern loomed above them. Jess made the dory fast to the rudderstock and stood up in the bows and reached for the sternports.

The windows were locked. No matter; he wanted elevation, not penetration. Using the sill for a handhold he stepped up on the top of the rudderpost, reached higher and got a grasp on the plank sheer molding and hauled himself up until his feet were on the sill, and then reached again and found the main sheer molding, and that gave him a boost up to the little larboard house's sternport.

From this position he could have slipped easily into the alleyway between the two houses and presented himself at the rear of Starr's men. But he chose to go on up to the stern roof. An armed man has a great physical and psychological advantage over his enemy when he is standing securely above him.

Grimacing with exertion, Jess reached his left hand to the edge of the roof, got a firm grip, raised his right hand to join his left—paused to catch his breath—then straightened up on his shaky legs and prepared his strained muscles to complete the final haul over the edge.

A broad silhouette shifted across his line of vision and blacked out the dimly gleaming stars directly above him. And in that catchbreath instant a small round steel-cold object affixed itself to the center of his forehead.

He knew it was the business end of a boarding pistol, and he was dead certain about whose big hand was firmly wrapped around the other end—the end with the trigger and the cocked hammer.

"Come aboard, Mr. Hanna," Starr's voice spoke over his head.

14. Drowning Is Too Quick A Death

THERE WAS nothing Jess could do about it—unless he wanted to have his brains (*Such as they are,* he thought bitterly) splattered all over the floes beneath him.

Starr stepped back and Jess hauled himself over the edge of the frost-glaced roof. He heard Gant's voice in the alleyway below, calling down to Tavi.

"Drop them choppers, Kanaka. Or we'll splice your shipmate's bellybutton to his backbone!"

Tavi, as reserved and unemotional as an Easter Island statue, let his boat hatchets plunk to the floorboards of the dory. At Gant's command, he scrambled up into the alleyway. Starr herded Jess down the house ladder to the barricaded afterdeck. Levi Munson and Jekiel Burr grinned at him in the dark and flourished their muskets in his face. Starr shoved them aside and planted the barrel of his pistol in Jess's navel.

"Like a cat you are, eh my son? Neither spermaceti nor typhoon can deep-six you. Nine lives you've got, aye? But how will you trim ship with a cargo of lead in your bows, eh?" He gave Jess a vicious jab in the midriff with the pistol barrel.

Jess backed up against the larboard bulkhead and wet his lips but couldn't find anything to say. He was too stunned by the sudden reversal of fortune, too downright awed by the close proximity of death, to speak.

"You forgot about Nook, eh my son?" Starr taunted him, jabbing again with the pistol. "Forgot what he told us about the dory you had berthed under the bowsprit. I know you, Jumping Jack. I know your mind. If you miss stays on larboard, you'll try tacking on starboard. I figured you'd try to slip astern of us in the dory sooner or later."

Jess definitely did not want to die, but at that exact moment death seemed as inevitable as an ebb tide following a flood, and once a man comes face to face with an inexorable fact there is no profit in cringing before it and begging for mercy.

"All right, blast you!" he cried. "Then shoot. End it!"

Starr sneered in his face.

"Not quite that lively, bucko. There's still the Irisher

and that fool Meigs. Cover him, Levi!" he ordered the harpooner.

Starr stepped to the barricade and bellowed down the deck.

"Barnaby! Meigs! We've got Hanna and the Kanaka here. Throw out your arms and come aft, else I'll mince 'em like blubber!"

There was a prolonged pause. Then Meigs's quavering voice—"Hanna! Is it true? Does he have you?"

"Aye!" Jess called back.

A moment later a flensing spade, boat spade, a lance and a hatchet clattered on the deck abaft the tryworks, and Meigs's voice sounded again.

"That's all I've got, Mr. Mate. Barnaby's below with a busted forefoot. I'm coming out to larboard. Don't shoot!"

Jess, his back plastered to the bulkhead, lowered his chin to his chest in abject despair. The mutiny aboard the *Bunyan* was suddenly and tragically over.

"Take Jumping Jack and the Kanaka below and lash 'em down," Starr ordered Gant.

"What about Barnaby and Meigs?"

"Meigs is a gutless fool. He'll do what I tell him. I want him on deck to help get underway. Lash Barnaby where he lays. Jump now! I want this business over with by dawn."

Gant and Munson prodded Jess and Tavi down the after companion with their boarding pistols. Once in the main cabin Gant ordered Tavi to lie on his back on the table, and Munson lashed the Kanaka securely to the planks with a length of lance-warp.

"All right, Jumping Jack," Gant poked at Jess with his pistol, "tack up to the mast."

Jess put his back to the butt of the mizzenmast and Munson juried him to it, cinching up his handiwork with a snug bowline knot, muttering, "Let's see you jump out a this hitch, Jack."

"On deck now," Gant snapped. The two men started up the companionway, but Gant paused in the doorway to leer back at Jess.

"Don't flog the glass, Hanna. You'll have ice in your ears afore morning."

Jess said nothing, kept his face blank. He was trying very hard to assume some of Tavi's stoical acceptance of fate. Wasn't easy, though. His insides felt like the interior of a bobcat's cage.

Boots thumped across the spar deck. Minutes later the two prisoners felt a pronounced lurch in the bows, and sensed that the old *Bunyan* was slowly falling off to larboard, turning away from the land.

Aye, Jess thought, *Starr's slipped the cable and cut us adrift.* But why? Then he remembered what the mate had said to Gant: he wanted Meigs on deck to help get underway. *How can he do it,* he wondered. *How can he handle her when she's got nothing left but the mizzenmast and a mainsail?*

Then he realized that Starr wasn't going to handle her; he was going to let the old whaler blunder into the pack ice on her own. The big moment that Starr had long been awaiting was finally here. The time for barratry was now. He had told Gant he wanted this business over with by dawn.

Jess turned his head to the left. The chronometer

on the larboard bulkhead was ticking time away with unflagging insistence. One-thirty. Dawn was at five-forty-five. Four hours, and then . . . .

He strained at his bonds, but Munson was mighty handy with lines and knots. Jess felt as tightly wrapped as a mummy. He gave it up, mumbling to himself in vexation. Then he remembered Tavi who was lying just behind him, calmly staring up at the darkened skylight over his head—and he shut up. If the Kanaka could face death without a fuss, he should try to do as much.

A man should die with dignity, he told himself. Otherwise there's not much point to his life; because dying is the most important thing he'll ever do.

But thinking about it only made it worse. The truth was, he did not want to do it—with dignity or any other way. He started to wiggle frantically against the binding ropes.

There was a squeak of blocks and a squeal of running lines overhead, and a bellow from Starr—"Lay onto that crojack, Meigs!"

They were making sail with the sparse canvas they could spread. The spanker was gone, but they could still mount the crossjack, topsail, topgallant and royal on the mizzen, and try to balance the trim with the main course and the spencer.

Jess looked at the chronometer. Two A.M. He wondered how Barnaby was taking it.

It was three-forty when boots clumped in the companionway, and the sheepish-faced Return Meigs came into the cabin with Gant and Munson behind him. They lashed Meigs flat on his back to the starboard bench just below Tavi. Gant and the harpooner tramped into the cuddy and started banging things about.

Jess angled his head over his shoulder to whisper to Meigs.

"What's happening on deck?"

"We slipped the cable and made sail," Meigs whispered back. "There's ice floes all over the bloody sea, and if Starr ain't mighty careful he's gonna ram a berg!"

"What's the course?"

"Due south."

Aye, south, Jess thought. Hull down into the pack ice.

"What's gonna happen to us?" Meigs hissed urgently.

"I don't know," Jess lied. He knew it would probably be one of two things: the *Bunyan* would drift deeper and deeper into the pack ice and he and Tavi and Meigs and Barnaby would die a slow freezing death—or she would collide with a berg and rip out her bottom and sink, and they would drown in the icy sea.

In the next hour they began to hear reverberant thumps and knocks against the hull. The floes were beginning to crowd the ship. And at four-forty-five Starr came below and grinned a white square grin at Jess. His arctic eyes glittered like sapphires.

"Snug are you, my son? Well, it won't be long." The mate laughed and went swaggering into the cuddy.

Gant had already gone topside, and Jess heard Starr speak to Munson.

"The water's the prime thing. Make certain it's fresh. I can sail from here to Borneo on half a cask of fresh water!"

"Aye, and the voyage will likely seem that long, too," was Munson's grumbled reply. "I'll state it plain, Mr. Mate. I don't like it—four of us in an open boat in this blasted ice pack!"

"We won't be in the ice for long, you lubber," Starr snapped. "A day at best. We'll have the current in our favor and the wind too, from the smack of it. Satan's bolts, man! A well-provisioned whaleboat with a spirit-sail could carry us clear to the Timor Sea if we wanted to go there! It's been done afore, you know. Look what Bligh did in 1789. Thirty-six hundred miles in a leaky open boat with nineteen men and no rations!"

"Aye aye, but he didn't have ice again him neither."

"Ice!" Starr sneered. "By this time tomorrow all we'll see is a few floes a blind lubber could miss. We'll be back at Macquarie by tomorrow. And from there it's only a four-hundred-mile hop to Auckland Island, and two-hundred more miles will put us on Stewart Island. And then we're at New Zealand."

"And then what? What does New Zealand do for us?"

"And then we sign on the first whaler for home. The west coast of South Island has more whaling stations than a man-of-war has staysails! Now belay your grousing, can't you? I know what I'm doing."

He did indeed, Jess thought. And with Starr's fortitude and daring he would probably pull it off. *He's won*, Jess thought bleakly. *He's going to eat his cake and have it too. Ship, crew and cargo gone; and the insurance money in his pocket.*

The chronometer said five o'clock. Dawn would be within the hour.

Munson began making a series of trips topside, carrying aloft casks, bottles, sacks of food, blankets, cutlasses, muskets and ammunition. Starr passed through the cabin, laughing at Jess.

"What's wrong with the mate?" Meigs whispered. "Never heard him laugh once afore. He acts a little batchy."

"I think he is," Jess muttered. "It's been coming on for a long time. He believes he can do anything, and he's willing to kill himself to prove it."

"You mean *kill us!*" Meigs's voice was like a dog's whimper.

Tavi said nothing, made no movement. Death meant next to nothing to him because he knew that a happier land—a sort of Polynesian Fiddlers' Green—was waiting for him, and that all of his ancestors would welcome him with *méarahi te ma'a* (plenty of tasty food) and with song and dance. No, he would not wait to starve or freeze or drown on the bare table in the cold cabin. He would will himself to death, a trick his great-grandfather had learned from Métua, the priest of Tané.

"*Tirara,*" he murmured. It is ended. "*Parahi orua.*" Farewell.

"Whatname you fella gammon?" Meigs asked distractedly. "What's the crazy heathen talking about, Hanna?"

"I don't know," Jess said. But he could guess because he thought he knew Tavi. *I wish I could say good-bye to Barnaby,* he thought.

There was a bustle of activity on the upper deck and the three mute prisoners heard the screak of blocks and running lines; and a few minutes later their trained senses realized that the ship had lost headway. She started a slight wallow, with the pack ice still thumping at her hull.

"They've lowered the mizzen canvas," Meigs said in a breathless voice. "What's that mean?"

Jess didn't answer. He was listening to the voices of Starr and Gant which filtered down the companionway and through the skylight—

"Fetch the axes! I want that mizzen down." Starr.

"Why?" Gant, incredulous.

"Because I said so, mister! We're setting her adrift, and I don't want any telltale mast sticking up from the ice for some long-nosed Yankee sealer to spot and to come tacking in here to her rescue."

"Have you gone batchy, Starr? All we got to do is bust some holes in her bottom and let her fill and sink. The chart says it's at least two-thousand fathoms deep here. Why set her adrift and take the chance of having her spotted?"

"Because she ain't going to be spotted in here if

she's dismasted! And because I don't aim to scuttle her because drowning is too quick a death!"

Jess couldn't catch Gant's next words, but Starr's reply rang out like a trumpet—

"That's the command, mister! The Jumping Jack dies slow. Stand against George Starr, will he? Well, I'll correct his course for him. I'm master here! This is my show, and I say he dies like a gutted shark!"

There was a static pause—and then Starr's abrupt bellow:

"Don't aye me that way, you son of a blubber cask! Who do you capstanheads think you're gawking at? *I know what I'm doing!*"

Minutes later Jess heard the *wunk-wunk* of axblades biting into the mizzen—and then the tremendous ripping tearing scream of a mast carrying away. Starr's voice raged again.

"Now look lively and get the starboard waist boat over! Crack when I tell you—or I'll hook you from keel to pole!"

"Oh, lordy," Meigs whined. "We're for it now, lads. He's setting us adrift in this frozen sea!"

Tavi was busy with his invisible gods, and Jess didn't know what to say. He slumped in his hands, wondering which appalling doom would overtake them first. Freeze or starve?

He listened to the scrape and scuffle of the midships whaleboat being run out and lowered on the starboard, and the shuffle and clomp of feet on the deck as the two mates and two harpooners prepared to abandon ship.

There was a new sound—a sort of quiet scratching gouging, as if someone were working metal against wood. It was right there in the main cabin. Startled, Jess turned his head as the captain's door swung noiselessly open.

Captain Coffin stared out at Jess with dull, rheumy eyes.

15. Tirara—It Is Finished

H E HAD completely forgotten about the senile captain! If the poor old mariner had flickered through Jess's thoughts at all, it had only been to assume that he was already dead and overboard.

At that Captain Coffin was not far from dead. At least he certainly bore a deathly aspect. Standing shriveled and hunched with one crabbed hand clutching the doorpost, he looked as helpless and feeble as an old sick dwarf. He cackled in his straggly beard and stepped haphazardly over the weatherboard and shuffled toward Jess.

"Starr locked me in there last night," he said in his harsh clacky voice. "Left me to freeze. Aye? Like you. Like all of you. Aye . . ." For a moment his mind seemed to miss stays; then it drifted back on course.

"Thought I was unconscious, he did. Didn't think I knew what he was up to! *But I knew.* Aye, I've crossed his breed afore. Barratry, that's his game. Lose the ship and harpoon the underwriters. I know . . . I know . . . "

He went adrift again, wandering aimlessly between the butt of the mizzenmast and the forward bulkhead, mumbling to himself.

"Captain," Jess said. "Cut us loose, sir. Captain? Captain Coffin? You hear me, sir? *Cut us loose!"*

The old man hove to like a ship set aback in a headwind and blinked bewilderedly at Jess. "Eh? Who are you?"

"Hanna, sir. The Jumping Jack, remember? Starr is going to set us adrift in the ice."

The old man's face lighted like a binnacle lamp.

"Aye!" he crowed. "The mate didn't know I keep a marlin spike in my dunnage. That's how I forced the door. Can't keep an old seadog down, eh? Means to lose the ship with me aboard. But we'll stop him, eh Jumping Jack? We'll foul his cable yet!"

"Aye sir. Just cut us loose!"

Captain Coffin veered away from him and wobbled toward the highboy, fumbled noisily through a drawer and came up with a knife. He swung back toward Jess with the naked blade in his small chicken-clawed fist, cackling to himself.

Steady as she bears, Jess thought apprehensively as he watched the approaching knife in the old man's shaky hand.

"Starr!" Gant's distant voice split through the Antarctic silence. "C'mon, man! We're ready to make way!" And the mate's deep-throated reply, closer at hand as if still on board—

"Got everything? What about the log?"

A pause ensued—evidently while Gant and the harpooners searched through the clutter of gear they had aboard the lowered whaleboat. Then Gant's voice again:

"I recall I left it by the wheel."

"You lubber-minded soger! That log's our passport to riches!" Starr's boots clobbered the deck, striding aft.

Captain Coffin hacked at the lines binding Jess to the mizzenmast, and Jess stepped aside and shook himself free of his severed bonds and, turning quickly, laid a hand on Tavi's shoulder.

"You fella Tavi walkabout altogether, savvy?" he said.

"*O vau?*" Tavi murmured. Who calls? Then he sheered away from his expectant gods and ancestors and opened his eyes and looked up at Jess and said, "*Méa maitai-roa.*" All is well.

Jess started up the companionway.

The mate and the Jumping Jack met head on in the darkened alleyway. For a brief moment they were both transfixed—Jess poised in the doorway, Starr rooted beside the binnacle. Then the mate let out his breath.

"I'm gonna ride you down as I would the main tack," he whispered, and he shifted to the left and cocked his hook and lunged forward. Jess stepped fast to the left and swung the door forward and Starr's hook hit it *whunk* in the upper panel as Jess pivoted to the right, by the wheel, and delivered a straight-armed jab to the side of Starr's head.

The mate rocked against the bulkhead with a deep grunt and ripped his hook from the wood in a small shower of splinters, and then straightened up and trimmed his massive body as he slowly raised his hook again. His eyes glared wildly in the binnacle light.

Jess shifted around the wheel and put the skylight between them. They glowered at each other across the wood-ribbed glass, and Starr bared his teeth in a deep animal-like grin.

"Stand by for a gutting, my son," he breathed.

Jess sidestepped to larboard along the skylight and out of the alleyway and onto the open afterdeck. Starr hulked after him like a predatory grizzly, his hook raised and ready and silvery in the starlight.

Jess assumed the boxer's stance, both arms out and crooked at the elbows, doubled fists straight up and leading with the left, guarding with the right. Starr hesitated, blinking at the young seaman's unnatural posture. But he had Jess in the open now and that was all he cared about.

He lunged forward with a rumbling growl, his whole body launching itself in one tremendous piledive, with that bright sharpended hook already starting its flesh-ripping downward swing . . . .

But Jess wasn't where Starr expected him to be. He pivoted on his right leg and left-jabbed Starr in the temple and sent the mate half across the deck and flung himself after him, animated by a savagery equal to his enemy's. The hook whisked in the air and tore the front of Jess's shirt from his chest and Starr's left started to pummel his belly.

The pain of the assault was blinding, but the deep hard blows steeled Jess to renewed efforts. He commenced to box Starr off, and he was just holding his own nicely when a sudden yell from Gant distracted him.

"Starr! What's wrong on deck?"

Jess's eyes must have flicked to starboard, because in that instant Starr rushed him and pinioned his arms in a clinch and slammed him *wham* against the bulwark and jerked his head forward and bit Jess's ear until it was nearly torn loose. One mad heave of Jess's powerful arms and Starr, strong as he was, was thrown clear.

Jess whipped an uppercut to the side of Starr's jaw and the mate's knees sagged and he reeled into the scuppers and lashed out a kick to stave off Jess's attack. Jess sidestepped and drove home a blow that sent the blood spurting from the mate's left eye, and in the next second he was all over Starr, hammering blows from every direction, forgetting all the arts Barnaby had taught him about fighting—anything to get his fists on Starr.

Absently, he heard feet pounding on the dark deck and heard a yell and then a shot and another yell. But it all belonged in another place and to other people. He and Starr were the only two that mattered; beating Starr was all that counted. This monster of a mate was an enemy of everything human, and in that red moment Jess knew a relentlessness, a capacity for punishment, he was never to experience again. He was an avenger, an avenger of every human being the mate had bullied and beaten and killed.

He rammed his fist into Starr's wet face and drove him crashing into the mizzen fife rail, and stalked him, merciless as a tiger, and hit him again.

But Starr, battered or not, was still as cunning as a ferocious wolverine and he capitalized on the opportunity. He pretended to weaken, to sag into the snarl of knotted lines and pins, and as Jess rushed him, he lashed straight out with his right foot—a wicked kick designed to break a man's leg. But his sight was blurred with blood and the slashing kick landed high on Jess's thigh.

The pain was splintering. Jess stumbled away, dizzy and nauseated, and missed his step and slammed into the deck. Starr lunged to his feet and leaped forward, his massive body landing on top of Jess like a brick kiln, driving the breath from him.

Jess's head rolled. He saw the clean glittery star smear high above, and saw the shining hook rise over his face as the mate's hate-mad eyes deadened with a cold ferocity.

"Right through the brain, my son!" Starr roared.

Something went *whuk* in the night and Starr's huge body jolted as if he were trying to do a backspring from a kneeling position. His hook clawed helplessly at the air—once, twice—and he tipped on over backwards, slowly, and sprawled face-down on the deck.

Jess tottered to his feet and stood over the battered

mate, staring down at the boat hatchet in the man's broad back. Tavi strode out of the dark alleyway and looked at Starr with a blank expression.

"Fella father belong me rest altogether now," he said.

Return Meigs was beside himself with excitement. He trotted aft with a musket in his hands, yelling at Jess.

"Hi Hanna! You seen me? Seen what I done? Gant and the harpooners tried to board us and I blasted bucko Gant smack amidships! Man alive, he sank like a stone! And you should a seen Munson and Burr lay to them oars! Roundshot couldn't catch 'em!"

"All right," Jess muttered. "All right, Meigs."

It was all over, finally, and now that it was he didn't want to talk about it. He ached from truck to keel and he felt sick and weary. He looked around the dismasted deck littered with great black clumps of standing and running rigging, and said:

"Get something to eat and then get some sleep. We'll all need a lot of both."

"Aye aye," Meigs said, grinning. "Me for the mate's berth. I've blame well earned it!"

Jess looked at the passive Kanaka in the pale dawn glow.

"Tavi, you killed one fella Jack Hay, aye?"

"*É.*" Yes.

"And Captain Morse was fella father belong you, eh?"

"*É.*"

Tavi stooped down and raised George Starr's limp

body, got it under the armpits and dragged it across the deck to the bulwark and leaned it, steadying it, there, and then caught it behind the knees with his free hand and raised the legs straight up and gave a quick shove and the body shot headlong overboard.

"Tirara," Tavi said simply. It is finished.

Jess went below to the main cabin and found a mirror and did some handiwork on his torn ear. Then he gave himself a bracer of rum and sat down at the table with Captain Coffin and ate some cold duff. The old man was cackling to himself.

"Starr didn't think I knew his game," he mumbled. "But I knew, I knew. I was biding my time." His hooded watery eyes glared fiercely at Jess.

"And I beat him, eh? I beat the mate at his own game."

"Aye, sir," Jess said. "You beat him."

After a while he took some food and drink forward to Barnaby, and told him what had happened.

"I figure Starr had Jack Hay kill Captain Morse on the *Bunyan*'s last voyage," he reasoned. "And somehow the news leaked out and Tavi heard of it, and I guess he started tracking the steward. Hay must have suspected that Tavi, or at least one of Morse's Kanaka sons, was after him—that's why he was so batchy with fear when he saw you and Burr and Tavi in front of the Commodore Mayo the day before we sailed."

"Fair enough," Barnaby said. "But why then did Tavi want to sail with us *after* he'd pitchforked Jack in the barn?"

"To get home again. He knew we were slated to cross the South Pacific on the last leg of our voyage. Probably figured he'd jump ship when we got into the Society Islands." Jess frowned.

"And speaking of getting home—we're in a devil of a fix; dismasted in pack ice with only three able seamen."

"Well now, the drift's in our favor," Barnaby said, "and if you can rig up a jury you'll be able to hold her in the wind. Then set a course due north and pray for the best!"

Jess wasn't satisfied with prayer alone. He needed to take a definite course of action. Tavi was good with a harpoon or an oar, but he knew very little about practical seamanship. Meigs was a fair worker when told what to do, but he was not very bright. And Captain Coffin was next to worthless.

Jess did, however, manage to get the old man to plot a course for South Island. The big trouble was, how would anyone be certain the course was accurate? The captain's mind was pretty far gone.

Daylight showed the *Bunyan* covered in a thin frozen mantle, with the ice on deck making a curve from the in-board rails to where it raised in hummocks over the hatches. Jess set Tavi and Meigs to work chopping at lanyards and running-gear until the dragging spars drifted away. That helped to stabilize her hull in the hollow of the icy waves.

Meigs found a barrel of salt lashed to the main fife rail and chopped into it. It was a treasure. Wherever they spilled salt on the deck the ice crackled and melted

and did not freeze again. Jess went aft and saw that
the rudder, though sheathed in ice, was free in its
movements. So they could hold a course if they could
manage to jury rig.

He judged the hulk was drifting about as fast as a
man walks, and if she would point with the wind she
would move faster. Which meant she needed more
pressure on one end and less on the other. He went
below and told Barnaby his idea and the Irishman
said, "You'll have to rig a drag. Give you less pressure aft."

Meigs fetched an auger and they bored four holes
in the rim of a heavy hatch cover, secured the ends of
lines to the holes and brought them together in a
bridle arrangement, and then weighted one side of the
hatch cover with iron, lashed the end of a cable to the
bridle and heaved the contrivance over the stern, pay-
ing out the line as the whaler drifted away from it.
When 100 feet of line were out, they made it fast to
the quarter-bitts and observed the effect as the line
tautened.

The *Bunyan* paid off and swung her stern to the
wind. She yawed right and left, but she kept headway. The three seamen went forward to see what they
could do about a bowgrace.

Lashing together a matting of mattresses, hawsers
and chains, they hung it over the bows at the cutwater
to defend the hull from the sawlike action of drift ice.
Next came the jury rig.

Using a fore-royal spar for a gaff, a main-topgallant
spar for a boom, they fashioned a mizzen-topgallant

sail into a fore-and-aft sail, and then lashed the main course spar upright to the stump of the foremast and gave this jury mast permanent support with backstays and forestays they made out of the running-rigging, and finally secured a single block with a long line pulled through it to the underside of the boom, close to the end. This was their block and halyard and with it they raised the jury sail.

The sail leaned, strained and filled, and the *Bunyan* went staggering through the water, sailing at a ghosting but consistent pace.

Jess and Meigs hurrahed their delight and Tavi allowed a flicker of a smile to cross his inscrutable face. Jess took the wheel and soon learned that he could make little improvement in the serpentine wake the ship left behind her.

"An eel would break his back if he tried to follow our wake," Meigs said, grinning. But it didn't matter. She had a course and she was on it. And somewhere far over the ice-white horizon there had to be land.

The old whaler sailed on, plowing determinedly out of the pack ice and into the wide empty sea. As if to free herself of a haunting evil, she captured a twilight wind and picked up speed, sailing on into the blood-red eye of sunset—to finish her last commission and to clear her final account.

16. Only One More Day, Me Johnny

IT WAS the spring of 1824 when the spice ship *Reese* put into New Bedford harbor and dropped anchor. Twenty-four hours later the district sheriff and a young seaman dressed in fresh dungarees and a new peacoat strode into Mr. Munro's chandlery office.

They could hear Mr. Munro ragging a mute clerk as they entered, and the young seaman didn't pause to knock on the inner door—simply threw it open and walked in with the red-cheeked sheriff close behind him.

Mr. Munro looked up from his desk with a vexed expression.

"Who do you think you are to come barging in here?"

"I'm Captain Hanna of the whaler *Bunyan*," Jess snapped. "I think you know Sheriff Packer."

Mr. Munro blinked owlishly at the two men, and turned to his cringing clerk. "Clear out, Weems." He waited until the clerk had closed the door, and then, in a low voice, spoke to Jess.

"Did you say the *Bunyan?* My ship?"

"Aye," Jess replied coolly. "She's neaped on the west coast of South Island, New Zealand—if that's any use to you. Captain Coffin and all her officers are dead. I assumed command of her in the Antarctic Sea."

The owl-faced man looked bewildered. He shot a hasty glance at the sheriff.

"Dead?" he murmured. "Mr. Starr is dead?"

"That's right," Jess said. "And I'm here to have an accounting of the *Bunyan*'s funds with you. Before Mr. Packer places you under arrest."

"*Arrest!*" Mr. Munro yelled. "What are you talking about? How do I know what you say about the *Bunyan* is true? I don't know you. You say you're the captain of the *Bunyan*, but I've never seen you before in my life. You're no officer of mine! Stab me, I've a good mind to lay charges against you!"

Jess smiled. "I've already laid charges against you with the maritime authorities. That's why the sheriff is here—to charge you with complicity in barratry."

"You infernal young scamp! I—"

"I have four witnesses in town who were aboard the *Bunyan*," Jess cut in. "Two seamen, Gypo Barnaby and Return Meigs, and two harpooners, Levi Munson and Jekiel Burr. We picked them up after they had abandoned the *Bunyan* and set her adrift in the pack ice. There was another witness, a Kanaka named Tavi, but Captain Ames of the *Reese* set him on Rapa Island during our homeward voyage. I have the Kanaka's written deposition. Captain Ames wrote it down as Tavi told it."

Mr. Munro's eyes started to look everywhere at once at nothing.

"Now wait," he murmured, "now wait just a moment here. I—uh—the captain, Captain Coffin, I mean—"

"He died shortly after we reached South Island," Jess said. "But before he did he was able to make out a deposition in front of three British officers off the cruiser *Regent*. Their notations and signatures are on his deposition. I have that paper, and I also have the *Bunyan*'s log which shows an unauthorized change in course made by the first mate who was acting under your instructions.

"*And*—" he continued, "the two harpooners that we rescued have made out depositions under oath and are now eager to explain their part in the barratry scheme to the maritime authorities. Starr told them you were behind the whole thing."

"Lies!" Mr. Munro cried. "You—"

"There's also my deposition," Jess interrupted. "If you'll think back you'll likely recall that I was the stableboy who overheard your plans in the Commodore Mayo's barn two years ago."

Mr. Munro's beaked face looked like a wax mask set in a fixed wince.

"Now—now see here, gentlemen," he began in a

wheedling tone. "I'm certain that if we discuss this matter in a rational mood, we can arrive at an understanding that will be advantageous to all—"

"No, Mr. Munro," Sheriff Packer spoke for the first time. "It's gone much too far for any *mutual* understanding, sir. The charges against you are complicity in barratry and murder. No sir! There are too many witnesses, too many depositions and facts against you for any form of collusion like that!"

Mr. Munro sagged fatly in his ladder-backed chair, the absolute picture of the defeated and resigned man.

"What became of the cargo?" he asked weakly, almost as an idle afterthought.

"Sold at a dockhead auction on South Island," Jess said. "I had the money banked in Sydney and have their draft for the amount. Some of the money went to pay the passage home for me and my mates on the *Reese*. I now want you to pay me and my shipmates off in full, and also to pass over the cash lays for the widows or families of every man who died aboard the *Bunyan*."

Wearing the expression of a weary old owl, Mr. Munro hauled a heavy leather-bound ledger from his desk drawer.

"Let me see your draft on the sale of the oil," he murmured despairingly.

That afternoon Jess walked into the taproom of the gable-ended Commodore Mayo and found Elihu Folger picking his teeth with a wood splinter.

Elihu gave him a casual glance—and then took a second look.

"Jess!" he gasped. "Jess Hanna, alive and kicking!"

"Come aboard, Elihu," Jess said, grinning. "How's business?"

"Can't kick, Jess. But crack me! Where have you been these past two years? By grabbit, you've up and grown a man!"

Mrs. Folger bustled birdlike out of the kitchen and clapped her bright agate crow's eyes on Jess. Her mouth snapped shut as if she had just caught a worm —but not for long.

"My stars! I'm amazed you'd show your silly face in here, Jesse Hanna. And you that walked out on us without so much as a by-your-leave! If you think for a minute you can march back in here looking for your job, you can just—"

"Belay that!" Jess roared in a quarterdeck voice. "You ain't talking to any stableboy now." He plunked a gold guinea down on the counter and waited until it stopped ringing before he said:

"That's for the best room in the house—if there is such a thing in this bilge-rotted hooker. Strike a light, woman! Make my berth ready!"

Mrs. Folger's mouth dropped to her Adam's apple and she gawked at Jess for a count of three. Then she gave a brisk nod, murmuring *Yessir*, and sent an excited call for the serving girl. She hustled away with her skirts a-switch. Jess winked at the flabbergasted Elihu.

"You need a stretch of sea duty, Elihu," he said, smiling. "Then you'd know how to fake down her temper."

"Jess, Jess," Elihu said, reaching for a bottle of rum. "How you have changed! What are your plans now, lad? Do ye mean to stay ashore?"

Jess stared down the long highly polished bar. It glimmered like a burnished twilight sea he had seen in the Tuamotus on his voyage home—a glint of sun on a far lonely shore. And in that moment he knew he no longer belonged where he was. He had slipped his cable and lost the land-drag forever. The salt and the flying spume and the haunting cry *Lower away!* were too much in his blood.

"No," he said. "I met a whaling skipper last night. He's looking for a third mate and he offered me the position. I reckon I'll take it, because . . . ." But how to put the far, clear, demanding call of the sea into words?

"So and all," Elihu said with a shrug. "But 'tis a hard, wicked, dangerous life, so they tell me."

"Aye," Jess agreed. "But you see—"

At that moment he heard the clump of a limping foot on the porch steps and a deep Irish voice singing:

"Don't you hear the old man calling,
Can't you hear the pilot bawling.
Only one more day, me Johnny,
One more day!
Oh, rock and roll me over.
Only one more day!"

And then Barnaby thumped into the taproom and grinned at Jess, and Jess knew he would never again have to attempt to explain to anyone why he was going back to sea. He had found a home.

Glossary of Sea Terms

ABACK To set square sails back in a headwind and lose headway.

ABAFT Any object that is behind another, such as: The try-works are *abaft* the foremast.

AFORE Any object that is before another, such as: The skylight is *afore* the wheel.

AFTERDECK The deck area used by the officers on watch in the stern of a vessel.

ALOFT Anything above the maindeck; in the upper rigging.

ALOW FROM ALOFT! An order to the men in the rigging to descend to the deck. ALOW: any place below the deck.

AMIDSHIPS The middle of a ship; also called MIDSHIPS.

AVAST An order to stop whatever is being done or said.

BATCHY Crazy; to act witlessly.

BELAY The same as AVAST; also to make a rope fast, such as to a belaying pin.

BINNACLE   A box or stand containing a ship's compass.

BOARD HO!   Warning shout when a blanket of blubber is about to be swung inboard.

BOOM   A long pole or spar used to extend the foot of a fore-and-aft sail.

BOWGRACE   A protective covering hung over the bow at the waterline to defend the vessel against drift ice.

BRISTOL FASHION   Everything in order and in place.

BULKHEAD   Any partition or wall on a vessel.

BULWARK   The solid rail above the level of the deck.

CAPSTAN   A large swivel device on the foredeck used for raising the anchors.

CARRONADE   A short, light cannon.

CATHEAD   Short, heavy timbers projecting from the bows to which the raised anchors are secured.

CLINGING TO THE WEATHERBOARD OF THE QUARTERDECK   Said of an old skipper who refuses to retire from the sea.

COUNTER   The underneath portion of a vessel's stern above the waterline.

CROJACK (CROSSJACK)   A square sail on the lower yard of a mizzenmast.

CUTWATER   The forepart of a ship's bow which cuts the water.

DEEP-SIX   To drown. Anything that has been lost or thrown overboard has been Deep-Sixed.

DOLPHIN STRIKER (MARTINALE)   A short, perpendicular spar under the bowsprit.

DUFF   A baked mixture of flour and water with raisins or prunes.

END OF THE TETHER   The upmost length to which a man can go.

FAKE   One loop or coil of a line.

FAKE DOWN   To lay a line down in successive coils so that it will pay out properly.

FANG   To prime something, such as: To *fang* the well pump.

FIFE RAIL   A square-shaped rail around the foot of a mast, for securing belaying pins.

FLEMISH DOWN   A line coiled so that each fake is on the fake beneath.

FLOG THE GLASS   Shaking the sand down in a sandglass in order to shorten the deck watch.

FO'C'SLE (FORECASTLE)   The crews' quarters in the forward compartment.

FOREFOOT   The forward end of the keel.

GAFF   The spar extending the upper edge of a fore-and-aft sail.

GALLY   To frighten. GALLEY is the cookhouse.

GAM   A talk or visit. "A social gathering of two or more whaleships, generally on a cruising ground." (Melville, *Moby Dick*)

GHOSTING   A vessel making headway when there is very little wind.

GREASY LUCK   To wish a whaler good fortune.

GROW SEA LEGS   To go to sea.

HAZE   To bully a seaman. "To punish by hard work." (Dana, *Two Years Before the Mast*)

HOOKER   An old or clumsy vessel; from the Dutch hoeker.

HOLYSTONE   A soft sandstone used to clean decks.

HULL DOWN   When the hull of a vessel is concealed by the convexity of the sea.

I'LL RIDE YOU DOWN AS I WOULD THE MAIN TACK   An officer's threat to break a man's spirit or body.

JACK   Every seaman was known as *Jack*. JACK PRY   A man who was "in Everybody's Mess and Nobody's Watch," meaning he was a poor worker but a nosy busybody.

JAVA (JAMOKE)   Coffee.

JUMP SHIP   To desert.

JURY   Any makeshift mast, sail, rudder, etc., used in an emergency.

LARBOARD (now called PORT)   The left side of a vessel, as you face forward.

217

LAZARETTE   A compartment near the stern used for storing provisions; frequently used as a brig for prisoners.

LEE SHORE   A shore toward which the wind blows. Any dangerous place or situation.

LEVIATHAN   A whale.

LINES   All ropes are called *Lines* on board ship—never *Ropes*.

LUBBER   A land lover; an awkward or green seaman.

LUFF   To bring a vessel into the wind.

MAIN COURSE (MAINSAIL)   The lowest sail on the mainmast.

MASTS   *Fore-* the mast on the forward deck; *Main-* the mast in the amidships; *Mizzen-* the mast on the afterdeck.

MISSED STAYS   A ship is *in stays* when heading into the wind and going about from one tack to the other. To *miss stays* is to fail to tack correctly.

MONKEY RAIL (FANCY RAIL)   The rail around the foredeck in the bows.

NANTUCKET SLEIGH RIDE   A harpooned whale swims off with the whaleboat in tow. A wild ride on water.

NEAPED   A vessel that has gone aground or has been beached, and needs a spring tide to refloat her.

PAID OFF BY THE BOOM   A seaman who has been deliberately shoved overboard by an officer.

PALM-AND-FID   Splicing lines or mending sail.

PAWL POST   The shaft of the capstan, located in the fo'c'sle.

PILOT FISH   A fish that leads sharks or ships. A person who butts in where he isn't wanted.

POD   A group of whales.

POOPED   When the sea crashes over a vessel's stern.

RAKE   The overhang of a ship's bow or stern.

SCUTTLEBUTT-RUMOR   Gossip around the water cask when seamen gather for a drink.

SHROUDS   Standing rigging; the set of ropes stretching from the mastheads down to the ship's sides, to support the masts, and containing the ratlines up which the seamen climb.

SLIP HIS CABLE (SLIP HIS WIND) To die. A ship slips its cable when the anchor is cut loose rather than raised.

SOGER (SOLDIER) Any sailor who shirks work is said to be *Sogering*; he is acting like a lazy soldier instead of an active seaman.

SPANKER A fore-and-aft sail on the mizzenmast.

SPAR A stout pole used as a mast, yard, boom, gaff, etc.

SPAR DECK (MAINDECK) The upper deck extending from bow to stern.

SPEAK (SPOKE) To exchange greetings with another vessel.

SPENCER A trysail, usually used as a storm sail.

SPERMACETI A sperm whale.

SPOUTER A whale or a whale ship.

SPUME Foam, froth, scum on the surface of the sea.

STARBOARD The right side of a vessel, as you face forward.

STARBOWLINES The men of the starboard watch.

STOVE To smash in the sides of a whaleboat.

STOWAWAY One who hides aboard an outgoing vessel to get a free voyage.

STRIKE A LIGHT To look alive and hurry to do a task; the same as *Jump! Crack! Hump! Shake a leg!* and *Start!*

TACK A ship tacks when it goes against the wind, by coming about (turning) and resetting its sails to catch the wind. A ship is on the starboard tack when the wind is on her starboard side.

TAFFRAIL The rail around a vessel's stern.

TOM PEPPER He was kicked out of Hades because of his fantastic tales. A liar.

TOPHAMPER The upper sails, lines and spars.

TOPSIDE The upper deck.

TRIM The arrangement of a vessel's sails, cargo or ballast. To *Trim Ship* is to balance her so that she sails on an even keel.

TRITON The sea god. He has the head and trunk of a man and the tail of a fish.

TUGGIN HIS FORELOCK In the old days a seaman touched

the forelock of his hair with his thumb and forefinger when addressing an officer. This was the accepted salute. It brought about the expression "knuckled his brow," also, "he knuckled under."

WAIST   The part of the maindeck between the fo'c'sle and the afterdeck.

WHIP   A rope and pulley on the mainyard used for hoisting or lowering cargo.

WING AND WING   A ship sailing with all her canvas spread, or with a sail extended on each side by a boom.

YARD (SPAR)   The sails are hung from *yards* on a square-rigged ship.

YOU'LL HAVE ICE (or Sand) IN YOUR EARS BEFORE MORNING   A sailor who expects to be wrecked.

Glossary of Pidgin English

The Kanakas of the South Pacific learned this peculiar lingo from the early English and Yankee seamen who visited their islands in the nineteenth century. It is properly called *Bêche de mer,* rather than Pidgin, or Pigeon, English.

Because of the limited intelligence of the savages who were to use it, *Bêche de mer* had a vocabulary of about fifty overworked words. The following are the basic words of the lingo:

FELLA   This word is joined to any object or living thing. "You fella boy," "One fella tree," "That fella ship," etc.

BELONG   Everything *has* to be related (has to belong) to something else. Thus— "One fella anchor" cannot stand alone; it has to "belong" to "that fella ship."

WALKABOUT   Anything that moves is a "walkabout." A seasick Kanaka will say, "Belly belong me walkabout too much." Or as Tavi said, "That fella whale walkabout too much," meaning the whale was too active, too ferocious.

WHATNAME   This is the great interrogation that can imply any manner of question: "What is your name?" "What do you want?" "What are you doing?" "Where are you going?" "What are you saying?" or, "Who the heck do you think you are?"

ALTOGETHER   This word simply adds emphasis to the verb, such as: 'One fella whale walkabout altogether" — "There is no stopping that whale." Or, "That fella whale stop altogether" —"The whale was killed quickly."

GAMMON   Means to lie, or exaggerate, or joke, or to talk too much: "Fella mouth belong you gammon altogether"— You talk or lie too much.

TOO MUCH   This is another descriptive term, but it does not carry as much weight as *Altogether.* "One fella shark" might "walkabout too much," but "one fella typhoon walkabout altogether."

SAVVY   I understand; you understand?

Author's Note

All the combat scenes with the sperm whales—including Nehemiah's tragic death—are based on authentic incidents recorded in whale fishery.

And the whale ship *Essex* was sunk by a sperm whale. This happened in 1820 in the South Pacific. Six months later a few skeletal survivors were picked up in an open boat off the coast of South America, some 3,000 miles away from where they had abandoned ship. It is a grim maritime fact that they had resorted to cannibalism to survive.

The sperm whale is not only an intelligent, shrewd, ferocious, vindictive mammal, but he is probably the whale that swallowed Jonah. The Bible tells us that Jonah was thrown overboard from his ship to pacify a tempest, and was swallowed by "a large fish" and lived in its belly for three days before he was vomited up. Yet for many years many modernists, plus certain oceanographers, have claimed that the Jonah tale is pure bunk—citing the fact that a whale's throat is too small to swallow a man.

True—regarding all whales *except* the sperm. The sperm is the only species with a throat large enough to swallow a human being—and one of them did swallow a man, on August 25, 1891. James Bartley, of the whale ship *Star of the East*, went into a sperm whale's mouth and was swallowed into the mammal's stomach, *and lived to tell the tale!*

This remarkable incident was authenticated not only by two dozen eyewitnesses, but by journalists and scientists as well.

Geographically, some names which post-date the 1820's have been applied to certain localities. This has been done for the sake of the reader's identification.

ROBERT EDMOND ALTER

The Author

ROBERT EDMOND ALTER left home at the age of sixteen, determined that he would make social work his career. At twenty, after working as a citrus picker and at a score of other jobs, which included being a movie extra, he found himself in the Army. By the time he had reached his early thirties, he was back to an ambition he held even before his fascination with social work: he would be a writer. Before his untimely death at the age of forty, Bob Alter completed many books for young people including WHO GOES NEXT, winner of the 1967 Gold Medal Junior Book Award of the Boys' Clubs of America. His adult fiction was published in national magazines including the *Saturday Evening Post* and *Argosy*.